My LITTLE BRONY

My LITTLE BRONY

An Unofficial Novel about Finding the Magic of Friendship

K. M. Hayes

Skyhorse Publishing

Skyhorse Publishing books may be purchased in bulk at special discounts for sales promotion, corporate gifts, fund-raising, or educational purposes. Special editions can also be created to specifications. For details, contact the Special Sales Department, Skyhorse Publishing, 307 West 36th Street, 11th Floor, New York, NY 10018 or info@skyhorsepublishing.com.

Skyhorse® and Skyhorse Publishing® are registered trademarks of Skyhorse Publishing, Inc.®, a Delaware corporation.

Visit our website at www.skyhorsepublishing.com.

10 9 8 7 6 5 4 3 2 1

Library of Congress Cataloging-in-Publication Data is available on file.

Cover design by Gretchen Schuler
Cover illustration by Amanda Brack

Print ISBN: 978-1-63450-676-2
Ebook ISBN: 978-1-63450-677-9

Printed in the United States of America

Chapter 1

IF MOM ASKED me to smile one more time, I'd lose it. I pasted on the best grin I could manage, but I was way too old for first-day-of-school pictures. Plus, I wasn't particularly excited about my freshman year in high school. If it was anything like middle school, I'd spend at least half of it hiding from guys wanting to stuff me in lockers. Mostly by hiding in my locker *before* they had a chance to trap me in there.

"Are you done yet?" I asked.

"Put your arm around Holly this time," she said, pushing me closer to my little sister.

"Don't make me touch Drew!" Holly whined as Mom draped my arm around her. She was eight years old. Her long, blonde hair was curlier than a pig's tail and her nose was as turned up as a piglet's. "He stinks!"

"Just. One. Picture." Mom's voice had turned stern. I could tell her southern accent was about to come out more, which meant we were ticking her off. "And if you don't smile, I'm a fixin' to keep you here cuddling all morning. So get it together."

I smiled. Holly smiled. Mom took the picture, clearly unhappy with it. She was about to ask for another. I could feel it.

"Are you happy now?" Finally, Dad interrupted the horrible family ritual. He'd been leaning on his prized truck looking at his phone while he waited for this to go down. "Me and Drew are gonna be late if you keep this up much longer. I gotta prep for my first class."

I tried to keep my face as steely as my father's, but my stomach turned something fierce. Scott Morris, my father, wasn't just any old teacher at Yearling High School—he was the football coach. A five-straight-state-championship football coach. Some of the boys he had coached had gone on to be NFL players and hometown heroes. He was like a god to people in our small Texas town.

But Mom rolled her eyes. She was never impressed with him like others were. "Be careful, Scott, or I'll make you get in the picture, too."

"Get in, boy," he said as he opened the driver's side door. "That's our cue."

I bolted for the truck, glad to be free but still dreading the upcoming day. Dad drove down our long driveway with a wave to Mom and Holly. The golden grass of late summer stretched out as far as I could see. Only our neighbors' houses dotted the landscape. Originally Dad had planned to keep horses on the land he had bought, but it had never happened. Mom said he was too busy to care for them, and I figured that had to be true since I hardly saw him.

The drive was quiet. The only sound was the radio playing the country station Dad always listened to. The *only* one he listened to, even through the commercials. Not that I expected him to talk to me—he was what people called "a man of few words"—but still, part of me wished he'd give me some kind of advice.

Yearling High wasn't even the school I was supposed to go to. It was in west Austin, and Dad worked there coaching football stars. My local high school was Roosevelt, a much smaller school in town. My parents wanted me at Yearling because it was supposedly better, with higher test scores and good extracurricular programs. But I knew the real reason they insisted I change schools.

As I sat there with Dad not talking to me, I swore I felt his disappointment in the words he didn't say. If I had been better at football—or any sport, really—would it have been different? Would we be chatting about games and plays and the upcoming season right now instead of pretending we were alone in the car? Probably.

It's not as if I hadn't tried to play. Mom and Dad had enrolled me in peewee football as young as they could, and I played until I was ten. During that time, I had broken four bones, had ten concussions, and even got kicked off a team because they couldn't take how bad I was. It hadn't even been a competitive league, and Dad's reputation hadn't been able to keep me in.

I was that terrible.

Mom had finally pulled the plug on my football "career" after I broke three ribs, one of which had punctured my lung. I still remember my parents' fight in the hospital hallway as I lay in bed breathing as little as possible since it hurt so much.

"I can't take this anymore!" Mom had said. "He's gonna get permanently damaged from this! What will it be next time? His spine?"

"Injuries happen," Dad had replied. "It's part of the game."

"Part of the game?" Mom's words had screeched angrily as her voice went up an octave. "He's been injured more before his first decade of life than half the pros!"

"It'll make him stronger."

"Are you insane? What will it take for you to see he is *not* going to be a football star? He's horrible! He's as bad today as he was when he was four. He's quitting. *Right now.* I will not let you do this to our son anymore. For both your sakes."

It probably should have hurt when Mom had said I sucked that bad, but as I lay there in pain, all I had felt was relief. I *was* bad. And I hated football. I hated it so much. I was always the smallest kid on the team, the one the other boys picked on and teased because I couldn't run as fast or push as hard. Even after I had quit, they tortured me for not playing, for being different. Football had made me feel weak my whole life, so when Mom said I didn't have to do it anymore, I had cried I was so glad.

But Dad . . . I think he's been mad at me ever since for not being what he wanted. Sometimes I still felt bad about it, but mostly I was tired. It was easier not to talk and just listen to the music, watching the fields turn into suburban Texas.

Yearling High School was big, probably bigger than my town's square, with a large marquee outside that said WELCOME BACK TO SCHOOL, BRONCOS! Students headed in, smiling and acting like they liked being there. Dad parked in a spot labeled COACH MORRIS and turned off the truck.

"Ready, Son?" he asked.

I blinked a few times, surprised. I seriously thought he'd get out and pretend he didn't know me. "Uh, sure."

"Let's go, then." He got out and waited for me. Then we walked together toward the school's entrance. When I sped up to lose him, to show him he didn't have to stick with me if he didn't want to, he kept up. I almost asked him what was up, but I couldn't do it.

"Coach!" A big guy said about thirty seconds after we entered the school. He must have been a linebacker on the varsity team, judging by the fancy leather YHS jacket and the fact that he was the size of a bear. "Good morning, sir!"

"Harvey." Dad nodded and held his hand out to me. "This is my son, Drew. He's a freshman this year."

The guy glanced at me for the first time, an eyebrow cocked. Then he held out his hand. "Oh, hey! Welcome to YHS, Drew! I'm Jake Harvey, one of your dad's team members."

"Right." I took his hand, trying not to wince at his killer grip. "Nice to meet you."

"Yeah." He smiled at my father, not me. "Well, I guess I'll see you both around. Better get to my first class."

"Don't want to be late," Dad said.

"Yes, sir!" Jake ran off.

This very same scenario with different football players happened precisely three more times before I got to my locker. Dad stood there waiting for me to work the combination, and I realized something super weird was happening.

"What's your first class?" he asked, a hint of nervousness in his voice.

"English," I said, the dots finally connecting in my head. He was following me around so word would get out that I was his son. Because if people knew that, I might not be bullied like I was in middle school. I knew that was why they made me transfer, but I hadn't thought Dad would go to such lengths. Maybe I should have been grateful, but I was only angry. "I think I can get there by myself."

His eyebrows rose, wrinkling his forehead up to where hair used to grow. "You sure, Son?"

"Yeah. I'll be fine." I'd survived up until now without his help. I didn't need my *dad* giving me street cred. This was so much worse than being *the loser* because now I was reminded that even my old father was cooler than me.

"Well, okay," he said, scratching the back of his neck. "Holler if you need anything."

"Sure." As I watched him walk off, I could hear the conversation he must have had with Mom. They knew

I had been bullied constantly. Even if I hadn't talked about it much, the black eyes had said enough. Living in a small town meant everyone knew your business, so word got around fast that I was the exact opposite of my esteemed father. It wasn't the "better school" they wanted for me at YHS—it was the fresh start, where no one knew what a loser I was.

I stared at the ground as I headed to class, and my face burned with shame. I was so pathetic my parents had to save me. What was worse? They weren't wrong.

Chapter 2

I GOT TO English in time to pick my seat. There were only a couple students sitting quietly, most of them in the front. The nerd seats. While I might have seemed like a nerd in middle school, with my small build and good grades, even the nerds had known not to be my friend. They were picked on enough, and they didn't want to befriend the guy who got it worse than anyone.

So I didn't take a front seat. Or a back one, where the slackers liked to sit. No, I went right for the middle by the window, hoping that would be inconspicuous enough. My goal in coming to Yearling was not to stick out in any way. Maybe I could be that guy people ignored. It would be way better than the last two years.

People filed in, but I didn't look up because eye contact was dangerous. That was when people started conversations. So I drew in my notebook to look busy. Well, not drawing, but writing "English" in cartoon-like letters for kicks. I'd never taken an art class—I just liked to doodle when I was bored in class. Which was often.

"Okay, guys, happy first day of school and stuff," a low voice boomed over the chatter in the room. I looked up, expecting to see your average high school English teacher, but this guy was younger. Still old, but maybe thirty at most. He wore jeans and a T-shirt with only a vague attempt at formality by sporting a vest over it. "Welcome to Honors English. I'm Mr. Rivera, and I'll be the one torturing you with the English language for the next year."

Some of the students laughed. I was tempted but didn't want to draw any attention and reveal that I thought a teacher was cool.

"Since this is your first class of the day, this is also your homeroom. Which is just a fancy way of saying all school voting and announcements and junk will happen here. Let's start with me butchering all your names as I call roll." Mr. Rivera held up a paper, cleared his throat, and intentionally mispronounced every person's name. It was hard not to smile at his weird pronunciations. As he started on the 'M' names, I waited my turn to see how he would butcher a name as boring as mine. "Ahn-du-roo Mor-eez?"

I was admittedly impressed at his creativity. "Here."

He glanced at me. "Coach Morris's son?"

Whoosh. I swore I heard that sound when everyone turned to look at me. I leaned back on the windowsill, wishing I could run right through the glass. Nodding was all I could manage.

People started whispering. So much for being ignored. How did my parents think this was a better solution? Coming to YHS meant *everyone* would know who I was, and worse, expect me to be just like my dad. Which they'd quickly find wasn't true at all.

"So you go by Drew, right?" Mr. Rivera continued. "Coach calls you that at least."

I nodded again.

"Cool." Mr. Rivera made a note on his roll and went on butchering names. No one else was asked if they were related to school faculty. Dad talking about me hung in my mind. I had a feeling I didn't want to know what he said; it was probably along the lines of asking Mr. Rivera to watch out for his pathetic son.

"Ski-lair Zoek?" Mr. Rivera said. No one replied, so people looked around the class. "Okay, okay, I'll pronounce it right. If you insist. Skyler Zook?"

"She's not here," a girl in a prim dress said. I hadn't caught her name because I had deliberately not paid attention. She flipped her dark brown hair over her shoulder. "Trust me, you'd know if Skye was here. She's impossible to miss."

Several students laughed.

I knew those laughs, the sound of cruelty in them. My insides squirmed from all the times people had laughed at me in the same way, even if this time it wasn't directed at me.

"Well, I guess that's—" Mr. Rivera started.

The door burst open and in tumbled a girl. My eyebrows rose as I took in her appearance. She was tall and lanky, but that wasn't why she took up the entire room. Her clothes were bright with colors from the rainbow—*all* the rainbow colors—and she wore a headband in her white-blonde hair. A headband with blue cat ears.

"I'm here! I'm here!" she said through short breaths. "Did you get to the end of the roll yet?"

"Skyler Zook, I presume?" Mr. Rivera said. "Otherwise known as Skye?"

Skye nodded. "Yup, that's me."

"See?" the prim girl said. "You can't miss Skye. Even if you *want* to."

More quiet, cruel snickering. I watched Skye, knowing how much this kind of stuff hurt even when you pretended it didn't. She tipped her chin up and stared back at the prim girl. "Exactly my plan, Emma. Better than looking like I'm going to church."

Emma scowled.

"Now, now, ladies," Mr. Rivera said. "Please save all cat fights for the second day of school. And not in my class, please."

Skye stomped over to the one empty desk right in front of me. That was when I noticed she also wore a rainbow tail. And above that tail was a backpack covered in bright cartoon ponies. I vaguely recognized them because Holly watched that show. My eight-year-old sister would wear a bag like that . . . so I could see why Skye, who was my age or even older, got grief.

Relief and guilt hit me at the same time. Relief because obviously YHS had a student everyone would definitely pick on. Guilt because Skye would be in the place I had occupied at my old school, which meant I was at least one step up. It was cruel to think like that, but it wasn't as if I could do anything.

I determined to ignore the blue cat ears right in front of me. Hopefully the pit in my stomach would go away eventually.

Chapter 3

LUNCH HAD BEEN the worst in middle school. Even when the jocks hadn't found me to pick on, it had been a constant reminder I was alone. My one friend in the whole world, Quincy Jorgenson, was homeschooled so he couldn't eat lunch with me. I'd spent most of my lunches hiding in the bathroom, an empty classroom, or the library to avoid people at all costs. If Quincy had been there, we could have at least hidden together.

But I was selfish to want him there because Quincy had Tourette's syndrome. He had been so bullied in elementary school his mom pulled him after second grade. I never got why people had a problem with him. His tics weren't even that bad. Mostly he flared his nostrils a lot and randomly winced.

So, with that bad history, my heart raced as I approached the cafeteria. I usually avoided the place at all costs, but Mom had opted for a longer picture session rather than making me lunch. She'd given me a ten dollar bill and that was it.

People often thought of cafeterias as a group of obvious social castes, which was partially accurate, but to me the people in the cafeteria or the commons *belonged* in some way. This mind-set forgot people like me, the castaways, who hid in the nooks and crannies of a school like mice and knew they'd be dead if anyone spotted them.

I kept my head down in line as the noise of a million conversations crashed down around me. I'd get my food, find a quiet place in the hall, and survive. At least that was the plan. But as I got out of line with my burger and fries, someone called, "Drew! Hey Drew!"

It probably wasn't me they called, but I turned like an idiot. I fully expected to see some other guy named Drew heading for the voice, but I recognized the caller—the first football player I met this morning with Dad, Jake Harvey.

He motioned for me to come over. I looked behind me, just in case I was mistaken.

"Yeah, you!" He laughed, but it wasn't in that mocking tone I knew so well. It was . . . nice. Like how buddies laugh together. So I headed over, not sure what to expect. "Hey man, you can sit with us."

"Really?" My voice cracked when I said it, and I wanted to die.

Jake didn't notice and pulled out a chair. "Yeah. Sit by me. I need tips on how to get on Coach's good side."

"You might have a better idea than me," I grumbled.

The guys at the table laughed like it was the funniest thing they'd ever heard. Had Dad put him up to this? I wanted to get up, but now I was here and everyone had seen me sit with them. Jake hit me lightly on the shoulder. "Dude, so he's always like that?"

"Pretty much."

"Damn." Jake took a big bite of his food.

I did the same, not looking at the people at the table too much. But I couldn't help noticing they were definitely older than me. And cooler than me. And bigger than me. Even the girls were tall and sexy and way out of my league. Not that I even had a league.

"Hey, kitty cat!" a guy at the table called. Skye walked past the table with her lunch and paused. He threw an empty milk carton her way. "Scat! No strays here!"

Skye had an incredible glare. She took a few steps forward, looking like she wanted to fight. "You know, they aren't cat ears. They're pony ears. From My Little Pony. If you're going to insult me, at least do it properly so you don't look like such an idiot."

I tried to hold back my smile, but she noticed it before I could wipe it off. Her eyebrow rose, as if she were confused to see me sandwiched between these football players.

"Burn!" another guy at the table said. "Pony Girl's got bite!"

"Screw you," the original insulter said to Skye.

"You wish." She whipped her hair back and out of the cafeteria she went. Skye might have had better comebacks than I ever did, but she still hadn't stuck around for too long. My guess was she didn't eat in the commons either.

"So, you play ball?" Jake asked as if nothing bad had happened.

I shook my head. "I used to, but I sucked."

"C'mon, that's gotta be too harsh." Jake's voice was easy. Kind, even. And yet I couldn't trust it. Not after how they had just treated Skye. If I wasn't the coach's son . . . "You couldn't have been that bad," Jake continued.

"I was in the hospital five times from football injuries before I was ten." I held my hands out in front of me. "And I'm still waiting for that growth spurt puberty promised me."

Jake smiled as he patted my back. "Hey, I was your size as a freshman, too."

I looked at him, skeptical.

"Okay, I was three times as fat as you, but I *was* the same height," he corrected. "People called me dough boy. Then I started playing football, and I grew a bit. All I'm saying is, it gets better, you know?"

"Yeah, I guess." I didn't get why Jake was being so open when I hardly knew him, but I appreciated it in a way. He was showing that he understood me, which I didn't expect from such a big, tough-looking guy.

"Maybe you could try again," he said. "Freshman team tryouts are soon."

And there it was. This was even worse than Dad telling his players to be nice to me. He must have talked some of them into convincing me to play football again, which was absolutely the last thing on the planet I wanted to do. Not that I knew what I wanted to do instead, but football definitely wasn't it. "Uh, maybe. Though I probably wouldn't make it."

Jake gave me a flat look. "C'mon, your dad's the coach."

"And he knows how bad I am. If he had any sense, he wouldn't want me on his team." Except Dad didn't actually have sense on this topic.

"You're funny, man." Jake finished off his milk and crushed the carton. He tossed it at the nearby trash and missed. "Good thing I'm not on the basketball team, right?"

"Right." As I finished my lunch, I devised a plan never to enter the cafeteria again so I wouldn't have to sit with them. It was too weird. I felt like I was being stuffed into a box I clearly didn't belong in, and I'd rather be on the outside than have to pretend to be someone I wasn't.

Chapter 4

I WAITED FOR Dad outside his special coach's office by the locker rooms, hoping he wouldn't ask about today because I didn't want to talk about it. Not that it was horrible—it was too *not* horrible. Except in a fake way that hadn't made me feel any better than the jerks at my old school had. I wanted to go home, but I was stuck here until he was done with whatever coaching stuff he had to do.

Guys spilled out of the locker room dressed in football gear, and I groaned. Of course he hadn't told me he had scheduled practice on the first day of school. But I should have known since they practiced most of the summer, too.

Dad stepped out of his office. He spotted me and stopped his march to the field. "Oh, there you are. How was school?"

"Fine." My answer for everything. Even when things were not fine. "So, you have practice?"

He nodded, pointing a thumb over his shoulder. "You could come, you know. Get to know the guys a bit. Maybe hand out towels and water—it's pretty hot out there."

My jaw went slack. He wanted me to go out there and play water boy? Was he serious? I almost yelled that his crazy plan to get me back into this world wouldn't work, but I took a deep breath and forced myself to calm down. "I think I'll just go to the library and read. I can do my homework when you have practice. When I have it, at least."

"Oh, okay." Dad put his hands in his pockets, looking down. "Well, I gotta get out there. Practice ends at four, so you know."

"Got it."

Dad turned his back on me, heading out with the straggling players. He slapped them on the shoulder and smiled, happy to be away from me and in his element. "Alright, boys! Let's get this season started!"

I sighed, letting go of the pang in my chest as I headed for the library. It was a pretty nice space with computers and shelves filled with books. The librarian smiled when I entered, happy to have a visitor. She stood as I looked around. "Can I help you find anything?"

"Got any fantasy?" The library had been one of my hiding places in middle school, and so I had started reading while I waited out lunch time. Good way to escape.

"Of course! Over there." She pointed to the fantasy section.

"Thanks." To my surprise, someone else was there. Someone I recognized. Emma, the prim girl from my English class who had dissed Skye, huddled on the floor with a thick book I'd read before—book six in a twelve-book series.

She looked up when she realized she wasn't alone and slammed the book shut. After she scrambled to her feet, she stuffed the book back in its spot. "Drew, right? Coach Morris's son?"

I held back my eye-roll. I would get that a million times a day now. "Yeah. Emma, from English?"

She nodded, looking to both sides like she'd been caught stealing. "Hey, uh, I know I don't know you and stuff, but could you maybe not tell anyone you saw me here reading that?"

"Why?" I couldn't help asking since it was just a book and not even a dirty one.

"Because my parents don't want me reading fantasy novels," she whispered. "They think those books 'harbor evil and darkness.' I'd be dead if they knew."

"Ooookay." I had heard of this before, but I'd never met someone whose parents were that serious. My parents weren't much for church-going, just on holidays and when my very religious grandma visited. "I will tell no one. Not like I have anyone to tell."

She smiled. It was a lot nicer than I expected after how she had sneered at Skye this morning. "Thanks."

I looked at the shelves, unsure of what else to do. It wasn't like I often found myself in the presence of a girl who read the same books—who wasn't looking at me like I was the worm of the school. "But one thing?"

"What?" Her eyes grew tense.

"You gotta finish that series." I smiled when she let out a breath of relief.

"I thought you were gonna blackmail me or something!" She looked longingly at the book she was reading. "Have you read it all?"

"Yup. Stick it out, though book eight is brutal."

She covered her ears. "Don't spoil it!"

Surprised, I heard myself laugh, something I didn't do much anymore. "I won't. Just warning, in case you want to give up on it after that. I almost did."

Emma slowly pulled her hands down. "Okay. Thanks."

"You're welcome." Awkward silence came after, since I had no idea where to go from there. Emma didn't seem to either and grabbed her book back off the shelf. I found one as fast as I could and left the aisle because it seemed weird to invade her privacy. It's not like I knew anything about her except her deep, dark secret of reading fantasy.

I took a seat at a table by the library window that looked out on the commons area. It was a nice spot, and I almost looked forward to doing my homework here while Dad did his coaching thing.

The book was okay, but I wasn't hooked. I almost wanted to go back, but I'd have to see Emma again. Was I expected to talk? What would I even say? No, I'd stay where I was and deal with it. I kept reading, hoping the story would pick up, but it wasn't the escape I wanted.

I found myself looking out the window each time a stray student passed. There must have been more than football going on since the school hadn't emptied like I thought it would.

That's when I saw the rainbow that was Skye. She was skipping and holding what looked like fabric, hugging it to her chest like a prized possession.

"You can't look away, can you?" Emma's voice came from behind me.

I turned to see her staring at Skye, too. "Yeah. She's interesting."

"That's one word for it." Emma sat down next to me, which I did not expect. "We used to be friends, actually, before she went crazy. Best friends."

"Crazy?"

Emma nodded. "We live on the same street and played as kids, but then she started watching *that show* at the end of sixth grade. She's been obsessed ever since. Turned into a total freak."

I sensed a bit more to it than that. "You weren't allowed to watch it, were you? My little sister watches it—I'm pretty sure there's magic in it, so your parents would be mad about that, too."

Her face turned pink. "Why would I even want to?"

I shrugged. *Because your best friend does.*

"You don't believe me. You think I wanted to."

I put my hands up. "I didn't say that. I just said you probably weren't allowed, and Skye didn't care and got into it without you."

Emma frowned, and something about it twisted my insides. She was kind of cute, if I looked past the frumpy dress. "Okay, are you some kind of mind reader or something? Because that's freaky."

"It's all the reading," I said. "When you read a lot, you learn there's always more to the story than what you see."

"Fair enough." Emma watched Skye as she disappeared down the hall. "But I still think you might be psychic. Or maybe a girl."

My eyes went wide. "What?!"

"Guys aren't that insightful." She looked me over, and I blushed. "And you're kinda short. And pretty. Like guys in a boy band."

I could not get any words out. What she said was such a mix of insult, and compliment, and truth, I didn't know what to make of it. But one thing I did know. "Trust me, I'm a guy. And you're really upfront for someone who begs other people to keep secrets."

She smiled. "I haven't told anyone what I told you. It's weird, isn't it?"

"Yeah."

She looked at the clock and jumped up. "Oh! My mom's probably waiting for me. She gets off work just after school is over so I always have to wait. See you later?"

"I guess." As she waved good-bye, my heart raced a bit. Did I just make a friend? Or was it something different? I couldn't deny I was much more comfortable talking to Emma than those football players.

And I think I liked that.

Chapter 5

I DID WHAT I always did after school—headed right through our west field towards Quincy's house. A barbed wire fence separated our properties with a big sign that said No TRESPASSING. Luckily I didn't count. Ducking under the wire, I headed onto Quincy's land.

His parents *did* keep horses and other animals on their acres. Clucking from the chicken coop, bleating from the goats, a whinny from a horse—all normal sounds at Quincy's place.

The huge, shiny ranch house was built in the style of an old farmhouse but with better plumbing and electricity. I stepped onto the porch and knocked.

"Oh hi, Drew," said Mrs. Jorgenson as she let me in without fanfare. She was much older than my mom, since Quincy was their youngest kid and the only one still living at home. "We were wondering if you were coming or not."

"Gotta wait for my dad to finish football practice now," I said.

"Ah, got it." She looked at me sympathetically, knowing the whole story as we'd been neighbors ever since I could remember. "Quincy's in his room."

"Thanks." I went for the hall, knowing my way around their house as well as my own. Quincy's door was propped open, and he sat at the edge of his bed with a video game controller in his hands. He mashed the keys, eyes intense on the screen. He liked to play games because he didn't think about his tics as much when he focused on them.

He caught sight of me. "Hey man! One sec, gotta get this boss down."

"No prob." I sat on the bed next to him, watching the fight go down. I often watched him play single-player RPGs. Mom didn't believe in gaming consoles, so watching Quincy was the best I could get. We played other games together, too, but I honestly liked watching the RPGs. The stories were actually pretty good.

"Yes!" Quincy jumped up after he beat the boss. Then he sat back down. Now that the fight was over, his nostril-flaring tic started—always in sets of three flares. "That was close. Looks like you survived school."

I nodded, the day still processing in my head.

His eyes narrowed. "Was it that bad?"

"No . . . it was, I don't know, normal?" I didn't have the right words for it. "Well, maybe what I imagine normal is for people who don't get picked on."

His wincing tic broke his confused gaze. "So it was good then?"

"Maybe? Though it all felt fake, I guess."

"Fake?"

I sighed. Quincy was about the only person in the world I talked to—really talked to about myself and my thoughts. So I launched into the whole story about how my dad had set me up with the football players to get me back into the game.

"Don't you think you're reading way too much into this?" he asked when I finished. "Maybe that Jake guy is just a nice guy. And maybe your dad only wanted to make sure you weren't bored after school waiting all the time."

I grabbed a controller, wanting to play something before Mom called me for dinner. "My dad would have ignored me if it wasn't a setup."

"But what if he's trying to fix things?" Quincy picked a two-player game from the list on his console.

"You have to be so damn levelheaded," I grumbled. But that's how Quincy was, always ready to give someone the benefit of the doubt. Even though he was homeschooled from a young age, he seemed to make friends way easier than me. I knew he had several within the homeschooling network. Sometimes they would hang out here, too, but I always left because I felt like I didn't belong with them.

It was weird how I felt like I belonged with Quincy but not when he had other friends around. He seemed to understand my discomfort and didn't get mad at me for not wanting to hang out with them. And he still always made time for me because he said he liked me best. Maybe it was dumb, or sappy, or whatever, but Quincy got me through the hell of middle school. I might not have survived otherwise.

I liked things how they were now, chilling out and playing video games. We joked around, and I told him about Skye and Emma.

"Whoa, you talked to a girl for more than a few seconds?" Quincy laughed as he knocked my character back and killed me. He pretty much always won, but I didn't mind. "And not for a class assignment?"

"Yeah, I still can't believe it either." A smile tugged at the side of my mouth again as I thought of Emma's caught expression when I found her.

"I always thought I'd be the first of us to have a girlfriend," he said. "I better get on this."

"It's not like that." At least I didn't think it was.

"But maybe it will be." Quincy and his positive outlook on life—he had totally missed the memo on the sullen teen thing.

I shrugged. Although I had talked to Emma, I still thought about Skye. Or maybe both of them, and how they stopped being friends over something as trivial as a cartoon. And yet I sensed they missed each other, maybe even needed each other. Like how Quincy and I hung out. It made sense for no real reason.

It was completely not my business and probably not something I could even do. But as I sat there in Quincy's room, feeling truly comfortable and myself for the first time all day, I wondered if I could somehow help Emma and Skye be friends again.

Chapter 6

EMMA DIDN'T TALK to me in English class. Ever. She didn't even look in my direction, but she glared plenty at Skye. After school in the library, I was her personal confession booth. She'd dump this random stuff on me about her life, and I'd nod while working on my homework.

I should have found it annoying, but it wasn't. Yet. It had only been a week.

Then there was Skye. She wore a different, brightly colored outfit each day with a set of matching "pony" ears, but I still thought they looked like cat ears. Word had spread fast about her, and even though she'd been a freshman for only a week, people called her Pony Freak.

And me? Well, I still hadn't figured out how to avoid Jake Harvey. I tried to make my own school lunch and sit by my locker, but he hunted me down and took me back to the football table in the cafeteria. So I had to watch them mock Skye every lunch period.

Neighing sounds on Tuesday.

Lewd jokes about how horses do it on Wednesday.

Grass thrown at her on Thursday, telling her to eat it.

On Friday they gave up on being creative and knocked her lunch tray onto the floor.

On Monday, after Jake sat me down at their table for lunch yet again, I braced myself for whatever I would have to witness today. I hated seeing them do that to Skye—it brought back memories of every horrible lunch period I'd experienced—and yet I stayed silent. Sometimes I thought about sticking up for her, but I was too afraid I'd get made fun of, too.

And while life wasn't perfect, I had to admit that it was nice not being constantly mocked at school. I hadn't realized how often I was on edge until I didn't have a reason to be. People would ask me something in class during a group discussion, and I'd prepare for my answer to be laughed at. But it wasn't. Some people waved to me in the halls, and it still took me a moment to realize a fist wasn't coming my way and I didn't have to flinch.

In fact, Jake was laughing at my "skittishness" at that very moment. He ruffled my hair like I was his kid brother. "You're like a little rabbit, dude. Calm down, no one's gonna hurt you."

"I am calm," I lied. It wasn't hard to spot Skye's hot pink pony ears almost at the front of the lunch line. My heart raced as she stopped at the cashier.

"Sure you are." Jake shook his head. "Anyway . . . so freshman tryouts are next week. You been practicing?"

I bit back my cringe. Jake had offered to help me practice a couple of times, but I really didn't want to. Since he wasn't getting my obvious attempts at avoidance, it was time to say it. "Look, Jake, you guys have been cool to take me in, but I'm not gonna go out for the team. Football is not my thing. Sorry."

Jake pursed his lips, taking in this information. "Then what is your thing?"

"I . . ." Had no answer to that. Football and injuries had been my whole childhood. Middle school had been the aftermath of failing something I was supposed to have been good at. I'd spent so much time surviving that I hadn't gotten to the bit where I figured out what I *wanted* in my life.

"Hey, Pony Freak!" someone yelled before I answered. Not even a football player this time, but a guy who wore punk clothes and sported a mohawk. I didn't know his name, but I was pretty sure he and his buddies had some kind of band. "If you're gonna wear costumes, can't they at least be sexy ones?"

The guy's friends snickered, and another joined in, "Do you wear pony underwear, too? How 'bout you show us?"

"Shut the hell up, Teagan." Skye kept walking, her head held high. I had to hand it to her—she was strong as iron. She made it look as if nothing fazed her, and so far she stuck to her passion even when it made her a target. I admired her for it. I definitely didn't have the guts to stand out like that.

Chapter 7

"SO MY PARENTS really want me to go to a private religious school." Emma had found me at my table in the library. She had her fantasy book out—now almost done with it—and she would randomly start talking about whatever came into her head while reading. "They think public school is poisoning my soul. They might be right. I don't know. I can never tell what is and isn't evil and they seem to know so clearly. What do you think?"

In the last week, I had learned that Emma's father was a pastor and her mother directed the church's choir. They were very religious, which I didn't have a problem with, but it was clear in everything Emma *wasn't* saying that she didn't share her parents' devotion.

"Well, I wouldn't do anything unless you felt strongly about it," I said.

"That why you're not trying out for the football team?" she asked.

"What?" I tore my eyes from my science home-work. People were talking about me? They knew who I was? Of course they did, but I had tried to pretend otherwise. So much for that.

She blushed. "It's just . . . people were talking about it in one of my classes. They heard you weren't trying out—everyone figured you would 'cause your dad's the coach."

This wasn't supposed to be *my* confession time. I didn't mind her telling me stuff, but I wasn't sure I wanted it to go both ways. "Yeah, that's basically it. I hate football. For a long time I pretended I didn't, but it got to a point where I couldn't lie about it any-more. Mostly because I didn't want to break any more bones."

She smirked. "That bad, huh?"

"Yup."

A flash of pink flitted across the window, and we both looked. Skye held more cloth, this time in a deep purple color.

"What is she even *doing*?" Emma said, bitterness in her voice but longing in her eyes.

I wondered the same thing. "You wanna go see?"

Emma's eyes went wide. "No!"

"You do. You've been dying to know," I said, hoping I wasn't just speaking my own thoughts.

She pursed her lips, looking out the window. "I can't. What if she sees us?"

"*Us?*" I pointed to myself. "I never said anything about *me* going. I don't even know her."

This was the wrong thing to say because Emma's face lit up with an idea. And I wasn't going to like it. "You should go! If you were walking down the hall behind her, she wouldn't even notice or care! Then you could see what she was doing and come back and tell me."

"What? No! I'm not being your spy!"

She stood up and grabbed my arm, forcing me to stand up. "Hurry! My mom's coming soon. It won't take you that long."

"I'll look like a creeper!"

"You will not." She pushed me towards the library door.

I sighed. Emma asking this of me gave me an excuse to do what I'd wanted to for the last week. I pointed at her. "You owe me."

"Fine! Go!"

And then I was in the hall heading in the Skye's direction. It wasn't hard to spot her cotton candy pink clothes as she rounded a corner and disappeared. I sped up my pace now that she wasn't in view. The halls were pretty much empty; one other person came towards me who I didn't recognize.

I turned where Skye had gone. The school was still a bit unfamiliar since I'd only been there a week. I hadn't had any classes in this area, and as I passed windows filled with splashes of color I realized why—this was where the art rooms were. As I peeked in a few windows, I wondered how I'd gotten into this at all. I *did* feel like a creeper, snooping around someone I had no business with.

She wasn't in any of the rooms anyway.

I was about to give up and tell Emma I lost Skye, but a sound echoed through the hall at that moment. I wasn't sure what it was except that it sounded like a machine, which seemed out of place for the art hall.

Following the sound, I ended up next to an open classroom door. My heart raced as I tried to see who was inside without being spotted myself.

It was Skye.

She was hunched over a sewing machine, her back to me, guiding fabric under the fast-moving needle. A moment later the sound stopped, and she cut threads off the fabric. When she held up her work, I realized she was making a dress similar to the other ones she'd worn.

So she'd made all those things? That must have been a lot of work . . . a lot of work to get mocked every day.

She grabbed a pincushion, folded the fabric over, and pinned it, completely immersed in her work. I found it fascinating and was a bit envious she had found something she loved doing so much that no other opinion mattered.

Because I watched her, I didn't notice someone else was in the room.

An older woman with short, gray hair popped into view. A teacher maybe? I jumped back, startled, and she smiled. "Can I help you, young man?"

"Oh, uhh . . ." Behind her, Skye had turned and spotted me. She did not look happy. "No, I was just passing by and heard the noise. I didn't realize what it was and was curious."

The woman laughed. "Never taken a Home Ec class?"

I shook my head. "No, ma'am."

"And your mother doesn't sew?"

I shook my head again, wanting badly to get out of there because now Skye stood with her arms folded. I had a feeling I'd be on the bad end of her biting comebacks if I didn't leave soon.

"Sewing has become a lost art." The woman sighed, looking back at Skye. "Well, not to all. Luckily."

Skye gave the woman a happy smile and turned her scowl back on me.

"Sorry to bother you, ma'am," I said, turning quickly to make my way back to the library. I got halfway down the hall before I heard footsteps.

"Hey!" Skye yelled.

My stupid feet stopped. I should have kept going—part of me wanted to. And yet another part was honestly too curious for my own good. I turned around, and there she stood in all her pink glory, the happy yellow and blue balloons on her skirt a stark contrast to her furious gaze.

"What do you think you're doing?" she spat out.

I looked to both sides, as if a good answer would appear to save me. "Um, walking?"

This reply did not improve her attitude. "Are you spying on me for them?"

Them? Well, I was spying for someone, but clearly she did not suspect Emma. So I ran with that. "Them who?"

"Your stupid little football team, duh." She pointed at me, looking me over like I was dirt. "You can tell them that sending the runt of the litter isn't gonna work. It's way too obvious."

I blinked a few times, connecting the dots. "So you think the football team sent me to stalk you and find more ways to make fun of you?"

She rolled her eyes. "Don't play dumb. I may not be popular, but even I know who you are and what side you're on. Go tell your buddies to leave me the hell alone, okay?"

Skye stomped off without waiting for my reply.

I was stunned. Hurt, even. Not because she was totally wrong, but because she saw me as one of the bullies. Me. The one who was at this school because his parents wanted to spare him four more years of torment. I wanted to tell her I wasn't like that. I wanted to say I understood what she was going through. But it felt wrong when I had watched her get bullied and hadn't spoken up about it.

Emma found me before I got back to the library. "There you are! What took so long? I gotta go, like, right now."

"Got a bit turned around, sorry," I lied. "She was sewing in the Home Ec room."

Emma raised an eyebrow. "Sewing? That's it?"

I nodded.

"That's weird, though I guess I shouldn't be surprised. I didn't know she could sew." Emma grabbed her backpack straps, looking sheepish. "I gotta run, but thanks. See you tomorrow?"

"Yeah. Got nowhere else to go."

She waved as she headed for the school doors. I went back to my table at the library. While I tried to do my homework, knots grew in my stomach. All I could think about was how Skye thought I was a bully. Was I a bully by association? By silence?

Maybe I was.

And yet the thought of changing it scared me even more.

Chapter 8

FRIDAY NIGHT WAS pizza night at Quincy's house. I always made sure to be there. Good pizza was hard to get this far out of town. No one delivered, so Quincy's dad would drive out to get three large pies to last through the weekend. Mrs. Jorgenson did *not* cook on the weekends—said she deserved to have a break, too.

"I'm back!" Mr. Jorgenson called from downstairs.

"Sweet!" Quincy paused the game. We rushed downstairs, my mouth watering by the time we sat down in front of the boxes. The pizza was always a tad cold, but it never mattered because it was the good, greasy stuff, not a frozen or homemade pie.

After a quick grace, we dug in. Quincy handed me three pieces of pepperoni and sausage, my favorite, and grabbed some plain old cheese pizza for himself. He was picky like that, didn't like anything "too intense" in flavor.

I took a big bite. No matter how many pizza Fridays I crashed, I never got tired of it. "Mmm, thanks for having me again."

Mrs. Jorgenson smiled. "Of course, Drew. Wouldn't be the same without you."

"We're used to feeding all our boys," Mr. Jorgenson said. Quincy had three older brothers, two who were now married. "It'd be mighty lonely without you."

"For reals," Quincy said through a bite.

It was weird how I felt more at home at the Jorgensons' than at my own house. I honestly didn't even know what my parents and Holly did when I was here eating pizza and playing games with Quincy.

I was about to bite into my third slice when my cell phone rang. Pulling it out of my pocket, I stared at the screen in confusion. "It's my dad."

Quincy raised an eyebrow. "You gonna answer?"

I set my pizza down and hit accept. "Hello?"

"Hey, Son." My dad's voice was grumpier than usual. "So we just got a call from Holly's sitter. She got a job and isn't sitting anymore. We need you to come home and watch your sister."

"What?" I babysat Holly once right after I'd turned thirteen. By the end of the night we'd torn the house apart fighting and my parents grounded us both for a week. "Are you serious?"

"Dead serious." He sighed, exasperated. "Look, normally we'd just stay home, but we have tickets to see a concert your mother doesn't wanna miss. So I expect you home in ten minutes, or you'll have *her* wrath to deal with."

He hung up, leaving me with the command and no chance to argue.

"What'd he say?" Quincy asked.

"I have to go babysit Holly."

Quincy's eyes widened. "Seriously?"

I nodded. "Come with me."

"Hell, no!" Quincy ticked at the thought. "Your sister is crazy. And she always asks about my tics no matter how many times I've explained it."

I sighed. Holly *was* crazy, an eight-year-old diva who thought the world revolved around her. She always tried to boss me around like I was four and not fourteen. "Aren't friends supposed to have your back?"

Quincy held up his hands. "Sorry. You can't guilt me into this."

"She's not that bad," Mrs. Jorgenson said.

"Will you watch her then?" I asked. No reply. Even she was afraid of my little sister. I stood up from the table, knowing I had to get home although it was the last thing I wanted to do. "If I don't come over tomorrow, call the police."

Quincy laughed. "Okay. Good luck."

"Yeah." I trudged back to my house. Mom and Dad barely acknowledged me with the rush they were in, told me to feed Holly something, and then they left for their concert.

I approached the living room slowly, hoping to get a read on Holly's mood before engaging with the beast. She sat on the couch wrapped in her baby blanket with her eyes glued to the television. It became my entire goal to keep her in this state for the rest of the evening—it was much better than *talking* to her.

I made my way to Dad's recliner because I figured if I sat on the couch, she'd complain about me sitting too close to her. It had happened before, even with three cushions between us. Sometimes I even *looked* at her and was in the wrong.

Her eyes flicked to me as I sat down, and they narrowed. "You can't change the show."

I held up my hands. "I don't even have the remote."

Holly immediately scanned every surface in the living room, spotting the remote and pouncing on it. She wasn't letting it go for anything.

I rolled my eyes. "Is that really necessary?"

"I know you won't like my show."

"Whatever." I settled into the recliner for what would definitely be one of the longest nights of my life.

Maybe I wouldn't even make dinner and let her starve if she was going to be like this. The overly happy music ended, and Holly quickly started the next episode on our streaming service. In that quick flash, I realized she was watching the very show that caused so much trouble for Skye at school—My Little Pony.

As the episode loaded, the screen said "S3: E4 – One Bad Apple." That meant Holly was in season three of this show. There were at least three whole seasons of these ponies, and who knew how many more?

The episode started with a tiny pony freaking out about meeting her cousin. Then it cut to this super peppy song about My Little Pony and friendship being magic and junk. My eyes were overwhelmed with the colors, but at the same time I couldn't look away.

Some of the ponies had these things on their butts called "cutie marks." Others didn't have them and got teased for it by the mean ponies. The new cousin pony didn't have a cutie mark, but instead of siding with the "blank flanks," she started being mean to them with the jerk ponies.

That pit in my stomach over Skye grew about ten times bigger—I was that cousin pony. Okay, I wasn't as mean as the cousin, but I could see the correlation. Although I tried to look disinterested, I watched in horror as the cousin pony, who was supposed to understand, tormented the little "Cutie Mark Crusaders." I silently cheered on the Crusaders as they planned revenge and then felt awful when the older pony told them the cousin had been made fun of in her hometown for being a blank flank, too. She had come to visit to hide from bullies at home.

Just like I had gotten moved to a new school.

Why was the show being so . . . so *real*? I hadn't expected to identify with any part of this cutesy, girly thing, and yet here I was, hoping this episode would give me an answer to my own problem.

The Cutie Mark Crusaders ended up saving the cousin and apologizing for turning into bullies themselves. They knew she had only been avoiding teasing. Then they made up and became friends. It looked so easy, but I wasn't quite sure it'd work out like that in real life.

Holly went on to the next episode, and then the next, with hardly a pause. It turned out the older ponies were the real stars of the show, not the tiny ones. They were friends, but they were different. It made me curious—what were the previous seasons like? How did they become such friends? Now that I knew the characters, I wanted to know more.

I stood up abruptly, realizing that I was into the show. I could not like this show—it was a show for *kids,* for *girls* like my obnoxious little sister.

"You hungry?" I asked Holly.

She looked at me weirdly. "Yeah."

"Nuggets?"

She nodded.

I went to the kitchen and turned on the oven. I could have microwaved them, but I wanted an excuse to be away from that show longer. I had to cleanse my palate was all. There was probably some kind of addictive property about the ponies to keep girls wanting to buy the toys. So I got on my phone and watched some dumb videos, but I could still hear the show . . . and soon I noticed I was listening more to that than the videos on my phone.

"What is *wrong* with me?" I whispered. In desperation to block out the ponies, I connected my phone to the speakers by the sink. Mom used them to listen to music while she did dishes. I turned on a playlist of loud country rock.

Before the first song was over, Holly stomped into the kitchen and turned the music off. "I can't hear my show!"

"That was kinda the point," I grumbled.

"What?"

"Nothing." I sighed. She thought I would hate her show, but here I was trying very hard to dislike it. "Look, can we watch something else for a little bit? You've been watching that for almost two hours."

"But it's the *best* show. And it's almost at the coolest part." She whirled around and went back into the living room.

I balled up my fists. I wanted to call her a spoiled brat, to take the remote and change the show, to eat all the nuggets myself. Why Holly brought out the worst in me, I didn't know. It took everything in me to put her food on a plate and set it in front of her instead of dumping it in her lap. Then I headed for the stairs.

"You're supposed to stay with me," Holly said in her whiny voice. "Mom said!"

"You'll be fine on your own." I kept going.

"Drew . . ." She whimpered, sticking her lower lip out and everything. "I'm scared to be alone."

I almost left anyway, but then guilt set in. Besides, if she told Mom and Dad I hadn't watched her, I would get grounded. After tonight, if I survived, I could go back to Quincy's and beg my parents *never* to make me do this again.

"You suck," I said as I sat back in the recliner.

Holly's smirk was seriously evil. She didn't say anything, just ate her nuggets and watched her show. But I could tell she enjoyed my suffering.

I tried hard to dislike My Little Pony. I told myself the pony Pinkie Pie was annoying, but she was kind of funny. The songs were horribly catchy. The stories weren't *that* great. It wasn't *that* cool when they fought evil with the magic of friendship.

But I lied to myself. Even as Holly drifted off to sleep before the "coolest part" (at least I hadn't seen anything that I thought was the coolest part), I wished I could watch more. If she would stay awake a little longer, until this one season was over, I'd be in a good stopping place and wouldn't be curious to watch more.

As it was, the temptation to take the remote and start another episode was strong. I stood up, tiptoed over to Holly to pry it from her hand while she slept. She gripped it tighter, and I froze. Then she relaxed and the remote was mine.

Was I really going to do this? Did I need to watch My Little Pony that badly?

Yes.

And no one was around, so who would know? I pressed the button to play the next episode, but as it loaded Dad's truck pulled up the gravel driveway. My heart jumped, and I quickly pressed the back button. If he saw me watching this on my own—I didn't even want to know how he'd react.

I got my butt in the recliner right before my parents came through the door.

Mom came over, smiling at Holly as she stroked her curls. "How did things go?"

"Fine," I said. "She just watched her dumb show the whole time."

"She's been really into those ponies lately," Mom said as Dad hefted Holly to take her up to her room. "It's adorable."

Adorable. I had a feeling if they knew I had enjoyed the evening way more than I had expected, they wouldn't use the word "adorable" to describe me.

Chapter 9

TO THE AVERAGE person, it probably looked like Skye had dressed fairly normally. She wore a jean skirt with lace at the hem and a country-style, button-down shirt with little apples on it. Her boots were worn brown leather, and her cowboy hat matched. The only thing was, the hat had peachy-orange ears attached to it.

I knew she was Applejack today, and I kind of wanted to kill myself for knowing it. And for thinking she'd done a good job capturing something Applejack would wear if she were a person.

I forced myself to look at my notebook and listen to the daily Bronco News. They announced stuff for Homecoming—the game day, assembly, dance, and all. I got this strange urge to draw a guy pony in football gear because my stupid brain had somehow latched on to the desire to imitate the My Little Pony cartoon style. I liked doodling, and suddenly I had a million ideas for pictures . . . of cute little horses.

I'd only drawn *one* pony over the weekend though. Just to get it out of my system. It wasn't even very good. And I couldn't draw one here where people might see it. So instead I sketched a football and goal post.

"Okay, guys," Mr. Rivera said, clapping his hands together. "We're going on a field trip. To the auditorium!"

Several students offered confused noises.

He held up his hands. "I know, I know, you were so looking forward to learning about prepositions, but the school counselor decided that, instead of visiting each freshman homeroom, it'd just be easier to have one big career planning assembly. And with Homecoming stuff coming up, it has to be today."

People groaned, myself included.

"I know, thinking about the future sucks." Mr. Rivera motioned for everyone to get up. "C'mon. It'll be over in just forty short minutes."

We walked in a vague kind of line. Friends chatted next to each other. Emma was with a girl named Mary, who I now knew went to her father's church. For the first time outside of the library, Emma glanced at me and my heart twinged. I wondered if she wanted me to walk with her or something.

But I couldn't. It would draw attention and seem random when we sat on opposite sides of the classroom.

So I walked alone. Skye's boots clomped behind me, bringing up the rear. For a second I worried she'd yell at me, but I was beginning to think girls would only talk to me when no one else was looking.

The auditorium was covered in green velvet. Chairs, curtains, and even the carpet looked like old trampled forest green. Sure, it was the school's color, but even this was overkill.

"Gag me," Skye said behind me.

I wasn't sure what she referred to, but since she was into fabric I wondered if she noticed it, too. Then I got worried about noticing it myself. Why did I even care? Why did I find myself noticing and caring and even *liking* the same things as Skye? She was the weirdest of the weird . . . it couldn't be my destiny to be a loser forever.

We sat with the other freshmen who'd been corralled to this "career planning" thing. A woman in a pastel suit stood on the stage, smiling extra wide. "Welcome, everyone! I'm Miss Overly, the school's guidance counselor. This is a very important year for all of you! It's the year people start to tell you that things 'count' . . ."

Miss Overly was painful to listen to. She had a sugary sweet tone to her voice that would have been better for Holly's age than mine. And she tried hard to make the whole "you have to get good grades and go to college and pick a career *right now*" thing sound like it wasn't a big deal, but it felt like a lie.

When I was a kid, thinking about what I wanted to be when I grew up was easy. I could say almost anything—fireman, president, pro ballplayer, superhero—and adults smiled and told me it would happen if I tried really hard. Now? I knew better. Not everyone was cut out for everything. They could still fail even if they tried hard. And more than that, people *judged* you based on your job. If I wanted to be a nurse, people would look at me funny. Musician? Have a backup plan.

And if I didn't know what I wanted to be? People would think I was a loser with no goals.

I kind of was.

"Here are some sheets to help you explore what you might want to pursue as a career," Miss Overly said, as some of the teachers passed out stacks of papers.

It didn't seem like there was much help to be had. One sheet was a list of potential careers. Another listed the highest paying, because *of course* that's how you determine what to do in life. There were some personality tests and correlating careers according to your score, which seemed hokey. Then there was a questionnaire. I started with that, since I hoped it might get me thinking logically.

What is your favorite subject in school? None.

Do you participate in any extracurricular activities? No.

Does your family own a business? No.

Is there something you have interest in but haven't tried yet? I thought about My Little Pony, about how I wanted to draw them like a total nerd. So I skipped that question.

What did you want to be when you were little? This question wasn't much better because I had wanted to be like Dad when I was little. I had thought he was the coolest person in the world with the coolest job. He got to play a game all day and people paid him for it. Except I hadn't been able to do what he did—I was awful at it.

This was a stupid questionnaire and no help. In desperation I moved on to the quizzes. They told me I should be a motivational speaker, an engineer, or a teacher. So that was super helpful and clearly a trend of no trend.

"Okay," Miss Overly said after several minutes. "Does anyone want to share what career they're interested in?"

No one raised a hand.

"Come now . . ." She looked over the crowd, and my stomach flopped because I knew she was about to call on people. "*No one* in this whole auditorium has an idea of what career they want?"

I shrunk in my seat. *Please not me. Not me.*

Miss Overly pointed in my direction, and I cursed. "You, in the cowboy hat, stand up. What career are you thinking about?"

A breath of relief whooshed out of me. I looked down a few seats at Skye, a full ring of seats around her unfilled. She stood, putting her hands on her hips. "I want to be a costume designer, ideally on Broadway."

Some of the people around me snickered. "More like a designer for *clowns.*"

"Maybe she could make costumes for *real* horses."

Miss Overly gave the look I'd seen before. The one that said she didn't believe Skye could do what she wanted. "That's a good dream to have. But it's one not many are able to achieve, so a backup plan would be—"

"It's not just a dream! There is no backup plan," Skye interrupted, a surprising amount of anger in her words. "Backup plans make you weak and lazy."

"Oh, well . . ." Miss Overly didn't have an answer for that.

"If you really want something," Skye continued, "you don't let anything or anyone get in your way. You try until you succeed. You don't let the haters get you down. That's what I'm doing with my life, and you won't talk me out of it."

Skye sat back down. There was utter silence for about five seconds before people started whispering. Miss Overly cleared her throat and moved on to ask other students what they had picked. She predictably praised the practical choices and the desires to go to college. Even entrepreneurship got more praise than any artistic venture.

No one seemed particularly motivated as we headed back to class to grab our things. I dragged my feet, wanting no one to see how much I hated every second of the assembly and wasn't any closer to knowing what I was good for.

Before I knew it, someone was next to me. Out of the corner of my eye, I noticed Skye. "Hurry up. You're going too slow."

"Only if you tell me where you get all that conviction," I blurted out. "I could use some."

She stopped walking. I looked back at her staring at me like I was even stranger than her. For a moment I thought she might say something because I had never seen her appear so vulnerable, even through the crap of the last couple weeks.

I wanted her to talk. So badly. Maybe she had the answers.

In the end she walked past me and disappeared into the classroom. The bell for class change rang, and she was gone before I had a chance to put on my backpack.

Chapter 10

QUINCY HAD OPTED for PC games today. He sat at his desk and intensely focused on a game. It was a pretty popular one with a team of five players who tried to kill the other team's base. I played it with him sometimes from my computer at home, but Mom didn't like me to play more than one game at a time since it might rot my brain.

Quincy's brain must have been a pile of mold at this point. Which I didn't think was true because he did all his homeschool work before I got off school . . . and then some. He was already in sophomore classes even though he would turn fifteen a month after I did.

While he was so preoccupied, I pretended to do some homework for history. But really I tried my hand at drawing Applejack. She wasn't *as* girly, so I figured it wouldn't be so bad.

I remembered she had freckles and a cowboy hat, and three apples were on her flank. But I couldn't remember her mane or tail. I tapped my pencil on my notebook, trying to recall. A braid would be logical with the country getup, and yet I was pretty sure she didn't have a braid. If I watched one more episode, I would see it. It couldn't hurt to watch one episode. Could it?

"Hey, Drew." Quincy quickly pulled off his headphones and turned to me. I jumped, closing my notebook in case he came over. He smiled. "Did I scare you?"

"I was concentrating . . ." I gulped. "What?"

His face lit up in a big smile, and his nostrils ticked. "Should I be a pro gamer?"

I blinked a few times. "Is that a real thing?"

He nodded. "There are pro teams for this game. There's like a bunch of them in America and all around the world. And they get paid to play video games. All. Day."

I smirked. I wouldn't be Miss Overly and tell him that a backup plan might be a good idea. He'd probably hear it a million times anyway. "Sounds pretty sweet if you ask me."

"It sounds *amazing*." He turned back to the computer screen. "You can't be pro until you're seventeen, so I have a few years to practice. Maybe I should start streaming, see if I can get a following or something."

"You could. What game? This one?"

He shrugged. "I'm not sure yet. This one is fun, but there are other games people play pro, too. If I put in that much time, I better really like the game."

I nodded slowly. "Makes sense."

"You really think I can do it?" Quincy looked down, but it didn't hide his wincing tic. I realized he wanted this but he was scared he couldn't have it. It made me think of Skye and how fearless she was in her choice. How did she do that? Even Quincy, who at least had some kind of dream, had doubts.

"Why not?" I said, and I believed it for Quincy. "You're already ahead in school, and you're really good at video games. You could probably graduate before seventeen and be a pro."

His eyes met mine again, relief filling them. "Really?"

"Yeah."

"I thought you'd think it was dumb," Quincy said with a short laugh. "I've been thinking about it for awhile, but I haven't told anyone."

"How long?" I had no idea he wanted this even though I'd known forever he loved gaming. It never occurred to me that he could turn that into a career.

"A little over a year, at least. I thought maybe the idea would go away, but it hasn't yet. It's only become something I want even more." He glanced at his door with concern. "It's just . . . you know, parents."

"Yeah."

"They'll want me to go to college even though I haven't been in normal school in forever. I don't even remember what normal school was like." Quincy started up his "sh-sh-sh-ing" tic, the rarest of his tics, which meant he was more concerned than I realized. He was worried his parents would be mad at him for wanting to be a pro gamer. Or maybe worried he'd have to go to college and he didn't belong there. "Sh-sh-sh . . . gah! Sorry."

I shook my head. "Hey, I get it, okay? I didn't turn out how my parents wanted at all. I'm already a disappointment at fourteen."

Quincy frowned, but he didn't argue about it. "How do you do it?"

"I don't know." I lay back on his bed, looked at the blank ceiling, and thought about my blank future. For the briefest moment, I almost told him that I couldn't stop thinking about ponies and drawing them. He had the guts to tell me he wanted to be a pro gamer.

But pro gaming and liking My Little Pony were not the same things.

So I said nothing. Because if I told Quincy and he decided I was too weird and lame, I'd lose the only friend I had.

Chapter 11

I COULDN'T SLEEP. Sometimes my legs hurt too much, all achy and sore. I hoped this meant I was finally growing taller, but I hadn't seen any results. More likely, I probably just needed a glass of water and some pain medication.

When I couldn't take the discomfort anymore, I dragged myself out of bed and down the stairs. The house was quiet with everyone else sleeping. It was peaceful, relaxing even, knowing I wouldn't have to face any of them right now. I grabbed a couple pills from the medicine cabinet, popped them in my mouth, and washed them down with a swig of water.

It would take at least thirty minutes for the meds to start working, and now I was wide awake.

A My Little Pony episode was about that long.

No one was awake to catch me.

I'd avoided it for awhile, but in that moment I was weak. One episode. I'd watch just one. I wasn't stupid enough to watch it on the TV where someone might see me. No, I'd watch it on my smart phone in my bed. It might be a smaller screen, but I could use headphones and no one would know.

I opened the streaming app and typed "My Little Pony" in the search bar. The show came right up . . . at season one, episode one.

My finger hovered over the play button. I originally had planned to find the season three episode where Holly had left me. But with the option to start at the beginning staring me in the face—to know how those ponies became friends in the first place—it was tempting to start at the very first episode.

But that would mean I was serious about this.

It meant I would watch a lot more than one episode.

I knew I shouldn't want to watch, but I did. There were so many things I *didn't* know about my life right now that I couldn't deny myself any longer. I would have to hide it—that wouldn't be too hard—and figure out later why this desire was so strong.

So I pressed play and watched Twilight Sparkle come to Ponyville for the first time. She was a loner and a bookworm who didn't even care about friendship, but she met Pinkie Pie, Applejack, Rainbow Dash, Rarity, and Fluttershy as she tried to get things ready for a festival. Then Nightmare Moon showed up and Princess Celestia went missing, so Twilight and her new friends left to save the day.

With the power of friendship.

As I watched episode after episode of Twilight learning about friendship in Ponyville, it didn't satisfy my need. It only fueled it. The show was funny, and smart, and even meaningful. I was learning new ideas about friendships and friends . . . and also finding myself craving to have more of them. That was new since for so long more people in my life only meant more potential for pain.

I smiled so often my cheeks hurt. While I felt a twinge of shame, I couldn't ignore how happy the show made me. When I let myself watch it and like it, I was at ease and my problems were a million miles away. I hadn't felt this way in ages.

I didn't want to let that go.

That's when I knew I would watch My Little Pony until there wasn't any more to watch. And then I'd watch it again.

Chapter 12

DAD TURNED OFF the radio about five minutes into our drive to school. Since we had forty minutes left to go, I didn't take this as a good thing. He must have had something to say, and he never had anything to say to me. Chances were it wasn't a *good* something. Looking out the window like always, I tried to pretend I didn't notice the silence. Maybe he would chicken out and keep up the routine.

It didn't work.

"So . . ." he started. "I can't help noticin' something."

My stomach hit the floor. Did he know about My Little Pony? I tried hard not to let it show—I only watched it late at night on my phone, only sketched ponies in my room, and never let myself reference it. But I hadn't had my phone on me all the time, and my parents demanded to know the code so they could make sure I wasn't watching dirty stuff. Maybe Dad saw my recently watched list. . . .

I gulped, wishing I could jump out of the car. "Yeah?"

Dad gripped the steering wheel, looking nervous. This was it. He was going to rip into me. "You haven't signed up for freshman team tryouts. You're my son and all, but you still gotta follow the rules and sign up."

I kept my eyes on the landscape, letting out a slow breath of relief. Not that I was completely at ease, but I could handle this much easier. "Dad . . . I'm not trying out."

There was a long pause. "Really?"

I turned to look at him, the surprise in his voice throwing me off. Was he . . . hurt? Did he really think I was trying out? This couldn't be happening. He had to know by now I'd never play football. He could not possibly still hope for that to change. "Yeah, really."

"Well, why not?" he said with the anger I'd expected.

I leaned back in the seat, wanting to heave an annoyed sigh. Maybe talking about how I'd watched almost all the seasons of My Little Pony would have been better. "Because I'm horrible at football, remember?"

"You weren't that bad. I've coached worse." He seemed to think this would make me feel better. "Your mom's just gotten in your head. She didn't like seeing you get hurt, but you would have gotten better."

Now I was the one with nothing to say. Mostly because I didn't know Dad held such a different view on why I had quit. It sounded like he had it in his head that Mom had forced me to quit because she couldn't stand the injuries. He thought it wasn't my choice; all this time he was waiting for the right moment to get me playing again. He'd never given up hope on me.

It was touching, honestly. Here I thought he hated me, but he didn't blame me at all and had this hope I would still turn into a football player.

Which would make it harder to dash his dreams.

Of course, I didn't have to. I *could* try out, and maybe he'd put me on the team. I'd be a real high school football player. Never mind that Dad was the coach and would put me on the team whether I deserved it or not. Never mind that everyone would know that. Never mind that I would hate every second of it.

The easier path would be to pretend I was that guy and not the guy I really was—the one who pondered important topics like "how did Princess Celestia and Princess Luna get their cutie marks, anyway?"

But I couldn't.

As miserable as these last years had been, I was *more* miserable when I tried to be someone I wasn't.

Now that I'd found something that made me happy, even if it was weird, going back to football would kill me. I was sure of it.

"You fall asleep, Son?" Dad asked after I'd left the conversation on hold for too long.

I shook my head. "I . . . I just don't know what to say."

His brows furrowed. "So you're not even gonna *try?*"

"I *did* try!" My voice was so loud it surprised me as much as my dad. But I kept going. "I didn't quit 'cause Mom wanted me to—she saved me from this conversation. Or at least I thought she did. Dad, I'm not just bad at football. I don't even *like* it. I can't try out feeling like that, I'm sorry."

"I see." That was all he said, and then he turned the radio back on. We drove to school without a word, and even when we got there, he didn't say good-bye or look my way.

I tried not to feel bad about it—this was how I thought our relationship had been for years—but I'd officially crushed my father's hopes and dreams for me. And I had done it by choice. I thought we were distant before, but as I watched him completely ignore me as he headed off to his class, I knew this was only the beginning.

****

When I sat in the hall instead of at the football table, Jake didn't come and find me this time. I pulled out my homemade lunch, figuring Dad had told the guy I was a lost cause and he didn't have to be my friend anymore.

It was a relief, and yet it also hurt. Maybe I didn't like football, but I liked Jake. He was funny and seemed pretty nice for a jock. I wished, as was becoming my habit, that real life could be like Equestria. None of the ponies liked the same things and they still stayed good friends. Logically, life should be like that—we should celebrate our uniqueness—but it wasn't and that was depressing.

As I ate my food, some people whispered as they glanced my way. They were probably confused. Or maybe they knew I had officially become uncool. I waited for the teasing, but nothing happened.

About a week after freshman tryouts, the whispering hadn't turned into mocking like I expected. Instead, it died down until it seemed as if no one saw me at all. No one waved. No one smiled at me. The only person who ever said anything to me was Emma—and that was after school when no one else was around.

At lunch and in every class, I was a guy no one really noticed. I didn't stick out in any way. I didn't shine in any way, either. I was just there.

It was exactly what I'd wanted all these years.

But after a couple weeks, it was lonely. Sometimes I thought I should reach out to someone, make friends like Twilight Sparkle had. Maybe I could eat with Emma and her group if I asked. But I chickened out and went back to my spot in the hall. I sketched ponies and thought about the show I'd become obsessed with, wishing for the kind of friendship I watched unfold each episode and not knowing how, exactly, to find the courage to go out and get it.

Chapter 13

I KNEW MY love for My Little Pony was bad when I began having urges to share my drawings. I'd never wanted to share my drawings before. Even as I lay on my bed sketching Rainbow Dash, I felt it coming on. I'd drawn her eyes just right, and her hair looked perfect. Her hair wasn't nearly as hard to draw as, say, Rarity's, but I was . . . proud of it.

And that feeling made me want to see if other people liked it as much as I did. Except I couldn't show anyone. It had been a month since freshman football tryouts, and I was as alone as ever. Maybe even more so.

Quincy had gotten so focused on the pro-gaming thing that half the time I was there he barely talked to me. Not that it made me mad. I thought about how if I were in my own room I would be watching MLP and drawing. So half the time I did just that instead. Except I didn't tell Quincy why I wasn't coming over as much—my new interest wasn't nearly as acceptable for a guy as his was. Okay, it wasn't at all acceptable.

But I had kind of stopped caring because MLP filled the hole school left every day. Maybe I didn't have friends, but I tried to remind myself I wasn't bullied either. It wasn't so bad—I could come home, draw, and watch a couple episodes to beat away the sadness.

In fact, as I finished drawing Rainbow Dash soaring through the clouds, I realized I hadn't felt this happy in a long time. The picture looked awesome. I wished I were a little kid who could go downstairs and stick it on the fridge to show off. But I wasn't Holly, and no matter how good it was, my parents would freak out.

I still wanted to share though. I'd wanted to share the last four drawings—ones of Pinkie Pie and Fluttershy, of Big Mac and Apple Bloom. This desire terrified me on so many levels, especially because it wouldn't go away and was only getting stronger. I didn't know what it meant, but it would be the death of me whether I kept it hidden or gave in and shared.

This drawing was too cool. Maybe because Rainbow Dash was so daring, I got a bit daring myself. I opened an app on my phone I rarely used—Tumblr. I had made an account because Quincy told me it was cool, but it had never seemed that great until this very moment.

Because I could make a new, anonymous account. I could post my drawings there. Maybe no one would see them, but it would be like sharing in a way. And no one would know it was me. That would be the best part.

It surprised me how long it took to find an MLP name that wasn't taken. Clearly there were more fans than I thought. I eventually settled on A. J. Canterly: Pony Sketcher. I almost put in "artist," but I couldn't do it. I wasn't a real artist who'd taken classes and studied; I just liked to draw cartoons. I wasn't even sure cartoons were art—"art" brought to mind those stuffy painters and sculptors I had learned about in history.

I took a picture of my Rainbow Dash and in twenty seconds posted it on my new Tumblr with a #mylittlepony tag. I stared at it smiling, my heart racing as I thought about how anyone in the world could see this drawing of mine. Not that it was *likely*, but it was still possible and that scratched the itch of my desire to share.

Then there was a knock at my door and I instinctively shoved my drawing under my pillow. The door *whooshed* open before I even answered, and my happy feelings turned to fear. Dad stood there as I hurriedly tried to log out and change Tumblr to my other account.

"What're you doin'?" he said in a suspicious tone.

"Nothing!" I said too quickly. I held up my phone, showing my other account. "Just looking at my Tumblr."

He held out his hand for my phone, and I tried not to cringe as he scrolled through the content. He clicked the close button and tapped on another app. He probably suspected I had been looking at something a lot dirtier than My Little Pony, and I said a tiny prayer that he'd stick with checking my web browser and not hit the video streaming app where I'd recently watched pony episodes.

He looked me in the eye. "You weren't doing anything your mother would cry about, were you?"

"No . . ." I wasn't exactly sure *how* Mom would react to my MLP obsession. "Of course not."

"Good. You get a girlfriend if you want stuff like that." He handed my phone back. "Your mother says it's dinnertime and told me to come get you, so get downstairs."

"Okay." I headed out the door before him, confused about why he hadn't hollered for me to come down like usual. I sat at the table across from Holly, who was stealing berries from the fruit bowl Mom put out at every meal. Dad sat down at one end and Mom at the other.

"Did you guys talk?" my mother asked in her sugary sweet tone that meant someone was in trouble.

I raised an eyebrow, looking at Dad. Was that why he came all the way up? Mom had demanded that we have some father and son heart-to-heart? It made sense, seeing as we hadn't said more than a few words to each other since I told him I hated the very thing he had devoted his whole life to.

"We talked," Dad said.

"Yeah," I added. Technically, we *had* talked but probably not in the sense my mother wanted.

"Good. Let's eat." Mom handed me a bowl of mashed potatoes, moving on as if her mission had been accomplished. And like always, Dad and I managed to continue our silent agreement to thwart her attempts to bring us together.

For once, I didn't feel bad about it. I was too consumed with thinking about which drawing I might post next and what pony I might sketch tomorrow. Finally, I had something that was mine. I had to hide it, but it was mine and it made me happy. I felt free to be myself, even if I didn't know who I wanted to be yet.

And honestly, that was better than my dad's approval.

Chapter 14

NOW THAT I was in full drawing mode, I found a more secluded place to eat lunch where I could sketch ponies to my heart's content without risking anyone walking by. Oddly enough, that place happened to be at the very end of the art hall in a space on the wall where lockers were supposed to go but had been taken out or never put in. I fit there pretty well, and even if someone walked down the hall, they wouldn't see me.

I'd posted three more pony sketches to Tumblr, and to my surprise, I got a new follower about every day. Nothing amazing, but seeing that someone liked my drawings did something inside me. Whatever it was, it made me want to draw more, to share more, to keep going down this new path I found myself on. I tried to think of myself as a Cutie Mark Crusader—a pony still finding out what he was good at, what his "destiny" was. I had to *try* things if I was ever going to figure it out, not sit around moping about how bad I was at football.

I sketched Princess Luna since it was cloudy outside and she seemed to fit the mood. She was my favorite of the royal ponies because she didn't come off as perfect. She'd made mistakes—big ones—and I liked her for it. As I finished her body, I decided maybe this time I'd add a background. So far I'd only been working on the ponies and new poses, but today I imagined Princess Luna standing on a balcony looking at the moon. May as well make it happen on paper.

I wished I had colors. So far I'd been drawing only in pencil since that was all I had. It wasn't like I could drive myself to the store to buy colored pencils, and I was afraid to ask Mom to get them because she'd ask why. And I didn't have an art class or project for an excuse. Hopefully soon.

Footsteps broke my concentration. First one set walking fast, and then a bunch of stomping in the quick cadence of running.

"Get back here!" a guy yelled. "I'm not done with you yet!"

"Leave me alone!" This voice was familiar, but I'd never heard it so scared. It was Skye.

She screamed, and I heard a loud slam against the lockers. I carefully peeked around the corner. There were three guys—the tough punk-looking ones who I'd heard had a band. The one in front had Skye by the shoulder, and he used his other hand to pull her white Rarity ears from her head.

I pulled out my phone, scared at how far this had gone. But I knew from previous experience that *proof* was more valuable than Skye's words if she went to the principal.

"Give those back!" She reached for her headband, but the guy was much taller.

"Not until you say you'll go to Homecoming with me." The guy's smile was gross, the kind that clearly had dirty thoughts behind it. "You should be happy I asked at all, since the whole school thinks you're a freak."

"So I should be grateful an asshole took pity on me?" She scoffed. "No way. I might be a freak, but I have standards."

He shoved her into the locker again. "Why can't you just shut up and look good?"

To my surprise, I rose to my feet, keeping the camera steady. That guy was scary as hell. He could probably beat me to a pulp. But the way he talked to Skye made me angry. Not that I knew the first thing about girls, but I was pretty sure threatening them into going on a date was about the stupidest thing a guy could do.

"You want me to shut up? Fine!" Skye thrust her knee towards the guy's crotch, but he pulled back just in time. As if this wasn't the first time a girl had tried to defend herself against him.

"You wanna fight?" He laughed. "You think I won't hit a girl?"

I snapped. Not that I could fight the guy, but I had to intervene. I took a deep breath and cried, "Hey!"

They looked at me in confusion. Then they spotted the camera phone, and the guy snarled, "What the hell are you doing?"

"Just making sure Skye has video proof of your assault when she wants to press charges," I said, sounding way more confident than I expected. I wasn't even shaky. I was just plain mad.

The guy's eyes widened, his hands up in the air. "I wasn't really gonna hit her."

"You shoved her. Twice. I got that on video, too," I said. "Now give back the headband and leave her alone. Or I'll report you myself."

"Fine, man." He tossed the pony ears on the ground, snarling at me. "Who knew Coach Morris's son had a thing for freaks?"

Heat crept up my neck. Not that I liked Skye like that, but I suddenly worried they'd start a rumor out of revenge. Yet my mouth had a mind of its own today. "I don't have a thing for freaks—I have a thing for treating people nicely. You're the one who wants to go to the dance with her, but you sure have a weird way of asking. Might wanna try flowers and a 'please' next time."

He swore at me. "Whatever."

In a weird turn of events, he and his buddies walked away. I thought for sure I would be beaten. I always had before when I said the wrong thing at my old school. I breathed a sigh of relief, the reality of what I had done only beginning to sink in.

I had stood up for Skye.

People would definitely find out.

I would get a lot of flak for that, flak I'd enjoyed not having since I got here.

Skye picked up her ears and dusted them off. As she placed them back on her head, she stared me down like I was some strange creature. She said nothing, but it seemed like she wanted to speak.

I ended up breaking the silence first. "Are you okay?"

She narrowed her eyes more. "What do you think?"

"I think . . ." I knew what it was like to be surrounded by people stronger than you who wanted to hurt you. I had a feeling it was even more terrifying for a girl. "You're not as okay as you try to look."

She looked away, but I still caught her tearing up. "Why did you do that? Nobody tries to help me. Nobody cares if crap like that happens to me."

This was the perfect moment to tell her. I could say I knew what it was like to be bullied so badly you wanted to give up on life. I could say I knew why she loved MLP so much since I watched it, too, and it made me feel better than I had in years. But I couldn't do it. "It was the right thing to do."

"The right thing?" She laughed coldly. "Then why didn't you do 'the right thing' earlier?"

I looked down, ashamed. "I don't know."

"I do. No one was watching. That's the difference."

How I wished there weren't truth to that. But that wasn't the only thing. "Do I look like the kind of guy who can stand up to people without getting beat down myself?"

"I guess not." She walked away, leaving me alone in the hall with my drawings. A twinge of regret came, but I shook it off.

I couldn't share my secret with her. Not even another pony lover was safe. Because if she knew, she'd want to talk to me. As much as I wanted that, I wanted to stay un-bullied more.

Chapter 15

EMMA HAD STOPPED her confession-like thing after we'd been hanging out in the library for awhile. It might have been because she was on the last book in the fantasy series, and her eyes moved over the text so intensely I was afraid to even interrupt her.

I kind of wanted to ask about something. I mean, she had a secret she'd kept for a long time. Maybe she had advice I could use.

Because the longer I watched MLP, the harder it became to keep it to myself. I was halfway through watching the entire thing for the second time, and it was becoming part of how I viewed the world. I constantly had to keep myself from referencing it. And now I'd posted almost two dozen drawings on Tumblr. To my surprise, I had forty followers and some people even requested that I draw specific characters.

"Emma?" I said.

She glared at me. "What? This is a really good part so you better not be asking me some stupid homework question."

I smirked. It was funny how intense she was. "Would it really be so bad if your parents found out about your secret?"

Her glare turned to terror. "Did you tell them? Did someone else find out?"

"No!" I laughed even though I felt guilty because I would be just as freaked out if someone knew about my MLP obsession. "It's hypothetical. I swear. It's just . . . I don't know, it seems dumb to freak out over you liking books. Or freaking out over, say, someone liking a TV show."

She frowned. "You think it's dumb I'm not friends with Skye just because of that show, don't you?"

That was *not* what I had intended, but I guess it was better than her suspecting I was talking about myself. "I just don't get it is all."

She bit her lip, looking down at her book. "Honestly, I don't either, okay? I guess that's why I read this stuff anyway. Yeah, it's stupid that I'm not friends with Skye because of a TV show, but my parents told me I couldn't play with her anymore and I was a kid who had to listen. Now . . . I'm less of a kid and I listen less, but the damage with Skye is already done."

"And you really can't tell them?" I asked, wanting her to have courage and hoping it would rub off on me.

She shook her head. "If I did, I'd have to leave this school and go to an all-girls religious academy. I know I'm not some hugely popular girl or something, but I have friends here. I like this school and I like how things are. I don't want to lose that over one small secret."

Her words assuaged my own guilt about what Skye had said to me earlier. I didn't want to lose what I had either. Maybe it wasn't much, but it was the best I had had for a long time. But still, one thing niggled at my brain. "Isn't it hard to hide something that's such a big part of you, though?"

Emma went still, her dark eyes locked on mine. "You should be a writer."

"What?" I tilted my head. "Are you trying to dodge the question or something?"

"No, you just *think* about stuff. Like, a lot." She pointed to her book. "Writers think like you, asking questions and digging into characters to figure them out. That's how they make stories."

"How would you know?"

She shrugged. "Maybe I have more than one secret."

"Do you now? Are you a writer?" I had a feeling she was, and it excited me.

"I'm not telling." Her smile said everything. "But to answer your question: yeah, it was hard to keep it secret. It was getting downright unbearable to the point I thought I'd break. And then . . ." She looked away, her cheeks turning slightly pink.

"And then what?" I urged.

"Well, you caught me. And you knew. And I had someone to talk to about it for the first time ever. That made it so much easier to bear. You've . . . you've been a really good friend, Drew."

"Oh . . ." Now I blushed, too. She had called me a friend. Maybe only after school, but I would take it. I had a friend here who wasn't Quincy. Plus, she was a girl.

"I'm sorry I don't say hi in class and stuff." She played with her hair. "It's just that my parents would freak out if they knew I was friends with a boy. I'm not allowed to date until I'm sixteen, and I think they believe even being friends is like dating or something."

"I see." I fiddled with my pencil nervously. This was *not* the direction I expected this conversation to go. Not that I thought I had a chance with Emma, but it was weird even to talk about dating with a girl. "Don't worry about it too much."

But she looked worried. "I guess I'm one big secret of a person, aren't I?"

"A little bit," I admitted. *Except to me, which is weird.*

She laughed. "Okay, now be quiet so I can finish this chapter before I have to go."

I focused on my homework, but I kept looking over at Emma as she read. She was pretty and kind, and for the most part, I felt like I could be myself around her. I wanted her to be my secret keeper, too. She knew about the football stuff I had never told anyone but Quincy.

But I couldn't tell her about MLP. She'd probably stop talking to me since I liked the same thing her ex-best friend did. And I didn't want her to stop talking to me.

I had to find someone though. Emma said it made it easier to have one person know your secrets, and I needed it to be easier before I slipped up.

Chapter 16

I GOT HOME late every day, thanks to Dad's football schedule. With practices now going more than an hour and away games once a week, sometimes we didn't get in until way after dinner. It sucked, being stuck at school so long. We were almost home when my phone buzzed in my pocket.

It was Quincy. *You coming over?*

Still not home, I typed back.

Srsly?

Yup.

That sucks. Never gonna see you again.

I hadn't seen Quincy in about four days, which was a record. Even though he was focused on games, we still hung out often. But now that the football season was in full swing, I had no idea how long I'd be at Yearling High School each day. *I'm a prisoner to my dad's schedule.*

You need a car. And a license.

I wish. Dad pulled into the driveway, stopped the truck, and got out without even looking my way. I followed, still typing. *Just got home.*

You coming over?

Not sure. I'm starving. My stomach grumbled on cue. *Might be too late by the time I eat.*

True. See ya, man.

Yeah. The house smelled like something savory and salty, and I made a beeline for the kitchen. Hopefully something was still left from dinner. Mom and Holly were in the living room, and I barely processed Mom's greeting as I made it to the fridge.

"The blue container!" Mom called.

I grabbed it, threw it in the microwave, and waited the torturous few minutes for the food to heat up. In that time, I recognized the sound of MLP coming from the TV. I listened to the dialogue to see if I could pick out the episode. All the voices were the same, but I heard a word never used in MLP—"every*body.*" It was always "every*pony.*"

The microwave dinged, and I pulled out my food. I was dying to go in there to see what Holly was watching, but I didn't want Mom pointing out that I never hung out with them and why was I now?

"Honey!" Dad bellowed over the show.

"Coming!" Mom's footsteps went upstairs, and a minute later she appeared in the kitchen. Her smile screamed, "I need to ask you a favor."

"Hey, Drew, you going to Quincy's after you eat?"

"Maybe, why?"

"Your father . . ." She sighed, frustrated. "He needs to get out and I'm not about to let him go alone. He's just real hung up on the Homecoming game—can't lose, you know?"

I connected the dots. "So you want me to watch Holly?"

She nodded. "I know you hate it, but it won't be for—"

"It's fine," I said, knowing this was my chance to watch whatever MLP thing she was watching without looking suspicious. "She wasn't that bad last time. Maybe she hates me less now."

Mom smiled. "Thanks, sugar. We'll be back in a few hours at most."

And I was free to take the recliner and see what I was missing. I remained calm as I saw what was on the screen—it was Twilight, but *not* Twilight. She was *human*, at a high school, and her pet dragon Spike was a dog. I was so confused. Obviously I'd missed the beginning where they must have explained how this had happened. If only I could ask my little sister to restart the show. This was seriously blowing my mind.

"I'm *not* changing the show," Holly said.

I listened to Twilight, something about losing her crown and needing to find it? "That's fine."

I noticed from the corner of my eye that Holly looked at me weirdly. I froze, realizing I should have said something more antagonistic. She put her hands on her hips, tilting her head dramatically. "What's *that* supposed to mean?"

"Uh . . ." Even now, fearful that my sister had caught me, I found it hard to keep my eyes off the TV because I would miss the show. That's when I realized—and hoped and prayed she would go along with it—that Holly, obnoxious punk little Holly, could be my secret keeper. It was a risk, but she probably suspected anyway. "Can you pause it first?"

She frowned. "Why?"

I took a deep breath. Here I was about to confess to an eight-year-old, and my heart raced like she was Dad or something. "Well, because I don't want to miss it while I'm talking to you?"

"Huh?" Her face only deepened in confusion, as expressive as a living cartoon. Then it clicked, and her eyes popped wide open. "Do you *like* My Little Pony?"

I nodded slowly, waiting for her to laugh and tell me she would rat me out when our parents got home—to hold it over my head like the blackmail it was.

Instead, she smiled. "Really? You're not joking?"

"Nope, not joking," I said, unsure of what she'd say next.

"Who's your favorite pony?"

"Probably Applejack," I admitted. "Or maybe Princess Luna."

I didn't think it possible, but her grin grew even bigger. "You're not lying! Did you watch more or something?"

"I watched all the episodes." I pointed to the TV. "But not this. What is this?"

"Equestria Girls! It's the movies!" She bounced up and down. "I thought you were just a smelly, gross boy, but you like good stuff, too!"

"Movies, huh?" This was intriguing, and also odd. I was having a real conversation with my little sister for the first time ever. "So there's more than one?"

"Yup! You wanna watch 'em?"

"Yeah, but first . . ." I looked to the sides, as if my parents could hear me talking from miles away. Maybe it was stupid putting my faith in a kid, but I felt lighter having told her. "Can you keep a secret?"

She nodded, her curls bouncing.

"Okay, good. Because I need you to keep this a secret for me. I don't want anyone but you knowing—this is just a brother and sister thing. Can you do that for me?"

She frowned. "But why?"

"Just for fun." I hoped that was all she needed. "It can be our thing."

"Our thing?"

"Yeah." I went to my backpack and pulled out my notebook full of sketches. My palms got sweaty at the thought of showing her, but at the same time she was only eight. I could draw like crap and she'd probably still think they were pretty good. "Wanna see something?"

She stood up from the couch and skipped over. "What?"

"I . . . I started drawing them. Take a look." I opened to the first drawing and handed it over. Holly's eyes went wide as she paged through my pictures.

"Whoa . . ." she whispered with an odd sort of reverence. "You're *really good.*"

Her words caught me off guard, not because I thought she'd be mean, but because I didn't think they would hold such significance for me. My heart warmed at her sincerity, and I realized this was the first time any of my family members had ever said I was good at anything. It felt amazing, and I couldn't help smiling. "You think so?"

Holly nodded. "Will you draw Cadance for me? You don't have Cadance."

"Sure . . ." This was my window. I could feel it. "As long as you promise to keep my secret."

"I promise! Cross my heart and hope to die!" She pointed to the TV again. "What if you draw while we watch this?"

"Okay."

"You should sit on the couch so I can watch you." She sat down, patting the cushion next to her. I could hardly believe she was being so nice, but when I thought about it, she didn't have anyone in the house to talk MLP with either. So I joined her and she fawned over every line I made while we watched the first Equestria Girls movie.

"That's perfect!" She leaned on my shoulder as I finished up the drawing. "Thank you for drawing it. Thank you for watching this with me."

"No problem." And then it hit me. Holly wasn't as annoying as I thought—she just tried to get attention. Now that I thought about it, she was often left on her own while we went about our lives. She probably loved My Little Pony because they kept her company.

I decided then and there I should pay more attention to her because I had no idea hanging out with my little sister could be so fun.

Chapter 17

QUINCY AND I pressed the buttons on the controllers rapidly as we defended ourselves from the enemy team. But unlike my best friend, I had horrible aim and only got one player down before I ran out of ammo. Quincy, on the other hand, used four bullets and killed everyone. He smiled victoriously at the screen. "Nice."

"You're a god," I said, putting down the controller. "You don't even need me."

He laughed. "I do, too. You distract the team so I can shoot them."

"So I'm the bait?" Although I acted offended, I couldn't help laughing. If we won because I ran around like an idiot while he did all the work, I'd take it.

"Hey, you're pretty good at it." He punched my shoulder. "You don't die."

"I could be a pro not-die-er."

"Totally." He held up his controller. "Wanna go again?"

I glanced at the time on my phone. In truth, I was waiting for something big. Something I didn't dream of until Holly had made it possible. Turns out having her as my MLP secret keeper was the best thing I had ever done. She was like my supplier, feeding the fire with all things pony, encouraging me to draw and post them. She even said the other night that she was my biggest fan.

That's why she went to the store with my mom—to beg for colored pencils.

"Why do you only do pencil?" Holly had asked after I finished drawing Shining Armor to go with the Princess Cadance I had done for her. "The colors are the best part!"

"I don't have anything to color with," I'd told her. "I don't have that kind of stuff at school like you do, and I can't ask Mom to buy it without her wondering why. Then I'd have to reveal my secret."

Holly had jumped off my bed, bounced across the room, and disappeared around the corner before I had a chance to ask her where she was headed. But she had promptly returned holding a box of crayons. "How about these?"

"Hmm, I'll try, I guess." I hadn't used crayons since I was a kid, but I remembered them not ever coloring the way I wanted them to. They were too dull to make crisp lines like a pencil. Sure enough, when I'd tried to color a test Pinkie Pie, it was as bad as I remembered. "I don't think these'll work. Maybe colored pencils. Do you have those?"

Holly shook her head. "But I will get you some. I can ask Mom."

And that's why I was at Quincy's burning time while I waited for Holly to get back with things that would make my drawings even better. It was barely enough distraction. I was so eager to get my hands on something that wasn't a graphite pencil or a crayon, I could hardly take it.

"Hey, Drew." Quincy snapped in my face. "You there? Another game or not?"

"Oh, sorry." I looked up from my phone. "I might have to leave soon to babysit Holly again is all."

Quincy narrowed his eyes. "I thought y'all hated each other and she was a terror when you did that."

"Well, yeah . . . but she's grown up a bit." I fiddled with my controller, hating to lie. "And they started paying me for it. Money doesn't hurt, you know?"

He pursed his lips and winced. "Really? Because I think you're not telling the truth."

"What?" I froze, which probably gave away my guilt.

He pointed at me. "You're totally lying! Looking at your phone like that . . . being all distracted and barely coming over . . . you have a girlfriend, don't you? Which one? Emma or that Skye girl?"

"Neither!" I laughed, relieved that was the assumption.

"Then what is it? You're acting all weird lately."

"Uh . . ." Luckily, my phone rang right then. It was my mom's cell phone. I held it up for Quincy. "See? Not a girlfriend."

"This time," he said. "I'm still not buying it."

I answered the call instead of answering him. It was, in fact, Holly. "Hey, I got them. Come home, okay?"

"Got it. Be there in a sec." I hung up. "Sorry, I have to go."

I didn't feel guilty until I saw Quincy's expression. He looked sad, maybe a little mad, too. He knew I was hiding something, and my lying wouldn't change that. Should have known I couldn't fool my best friend forever.

"Yeah," Quincy muttered.

"I'll be your bait tomorrow, I promise," I said.

He smirked. "Good."

I ran across the field faster than I should have, considering it was dark outside. Only tripped once. When I got home, Holly was on the sofa and my parents were nowhere in sight. She hopped up, waving the bag like it was a trophy. "I got them! It wasn't even that hard!"

I put my finger to my lips. "Shh! Where's Mom and Dad?"

"Watching a movie upstairs." She bounced over to me. "Are you gonna draw for me now?"

"Sure. My room."

We headed up the stairs and settled into what had become a routine over the last several days. I'd lean against my headboard and prop my notebook on my knees, and Holly would sit next to me to watch. Tonight, she pulled out the goods, and I was surprised to find not only pencils but also a crisp new sketchpad.

"Whoa…" I picked it up. "Is this for me, too?"

She nodded. "You can't draw in that notebook anymore. The lines get in the way."

"Thanks, Holly. This is awesome." I wanted to hug her, but I held back. How could she be so thoughtful?

"Now draw me Twilight sitting in her library with Spike and Owlowiscious."

I laughed. Okay, so maybe it wasn't thoughtful as much as I was now her drawing slave. But I didn't mind. If she could get me this nice art stuff, I was happy to draw what she wanted. Besides, pleasing her was a good challenge. Sometimes she'd even tell me if

I was drawing something wrong—she made sure my ponies were by the book.

"It's the purple streak and *then* the hot pink," Holly said as I colored Twlight's hair.

"So purple on the left?" I held my new colored pencil on the paper, waiting for her approval.

"Yes. And pink on the right."

"I swear it's not always like that, but okay," I said, coloring in the right part. I thought about Skye, how her pony-inspired clothes got the little details right. "You know, there's this girl at my school I think you'd like. She dresses up as a pony every single day, wears pony ears and everything, like in Equestria Girls."

"Really?" Holly squeaked. "What's her name?"

"Skye." When I focused on drawing, it was shockingly easy to tell Holly things. Besides, she always had something funny to say. She was actually a pretty entertaining kid.

"She even has a name that could be for a Pegasus!" Holly clasped her hands together. "What does she look like?"

"Well . . ." My face got warm as I thought about her. "She's got blonde hair, and she's taller than me."

"Is she pretty?"

"Yeah, I think so." I gulped. It was the truth, but it felt weird to say it out loud. There was something about her I liked, even if I hardly knew her. It made me feel a little guilty because there was also Emma, who I did know and thought was pretty too. "But you know what?"

"What?" Holly leaned into me a bit to see the picture better.

"People at school aren't very nice to her. They pick on her a lot, like how Diamond Tiara and Silver Spoon pick on the Cutie Mark Crusaders." I grabbed a dark blue pencil. Holly had gotten Mom to buy a pretty nice set of pencils with lots of different colors—she had a way of getting more from my parents than I ever could.

"What?" Holly sprung up, looking appalled by the information. "Why?"

"Because they think she's too old to like My Little Pony, I guess," I said. "And maybe because she sticks out, so it's easy for everyone to make fun of her."

Holly frowned, thinking about it. "That's mean."

"It's really mean." I now saw why Emma couldn't stop telling me her problems. It was nice to say out loud that I thought people treated Skye unfairly. "Sometimes I wish Twilight Sparkle and her friends were around to fix it and help everyone be nice."

"You stand up to the bullies, though, right? Because Skye is your friend."

My pencil stopped, and I looked at Holly. She had her hands on her knees, her intense eyes on me. The hope in them . . . it made me feel horrible. She wanted to see me as the hero, but I wasn't. "Actually, Skye and I aren't really friends."

"Why not?" Her voice had grown angry. "You have to be her friend! She sounds awesome!"

I let out a long sigh. How could I explain it to Holly? An eight-year-old wouldn't get how it wasn't that easy for me. I didn't want to be the one to break it to her that the world sucked a lot of the time. "You know how I said Skye gets teased? What do you think would happen if I told people I liked ponies, too?"

This did not improve Holly's expression. "Why would people make fun of you guys for liking ponies? It's the best show in the world! Those people are stupid. You should tell all of them they're stupid."

I let out a dry laugh. Holly and Skye would get along perfectly. I wanted to refute her, but my little sister had a point. "I wish I was as brave as you."

"Just do what Rainbow Dash would do," Holly said. "Dash wouldn't leave Skye alone like that. She's loyal. Just like I'm loyal to you because you like ponies, too."

Everything snapped into place in my head. Silly little Holly, giving me a lecture about friendship. I should have been smart enough to see it myself, but it took this to make me realize that if I wanted the kind of friendships in My Little Pony, I needed to be more like the ponies.

Honesty, loyalty, laughter, generosity, kindness . . . magic.

I couldn't hide forever. I decided right then that I would tell Skye I liked MLP, too. That was the first step. The biggest, scariest, step.

Chapter 18

I WAITED NERVOUSLY in English for Skye to show up. It was the only class I had with her, and she sat right in front of me. There was no better time to ask her if she might want to hang out with me at lunch.

I had worked it out in my head. If I asked her to have lunch with me, she *might* do it. She knew I sat out in the middle of nowhere now—a place where people wouldn't bother her. Maybe she realized I wasn't the enemy. Then I could tell her I was an MLP fan with no one around. We could talk ponies and be friends and stuff. It would be the best of both worlds.

But, as usual, Skye wasn't there yet. The late bell was about to ring, and my heart pounded. If she didn't get here soon, class would start and it'd be a lot harder to talk to her. At the very last minute, in she came, sprinting to her desk in a whirl of pastels. She was Princess Celestia today.

Mr. Rivera gathered his things at his desk, ready to stand up and start class. I didn't have time to think about it more, so I tapped on Skye's shoulder once and tried not to freak out.

She didn't turn around.

So I tried again, this time daring to say, "Hey, Skye."

"What?" She turned around, immediately on the defensive.

"I just wanted to ask—" The late bell rang.

Mr. Rivera cleared his throat, and my chance was gone. Skye turned back around with an eye-roll, and Mr. Rivera began collecting homework. He took roll and by then the morning announcements were on. Maybe, if I was lucky, I'd have a chance to ask Skye after class.

"Homecoming is this weekend, guys!" said the smiley announcer girl on the screen. "I hope you're all as excited as I am! The dance will be—"

"The dance?" the guy announcer said. "Forget the dance! It's all about the football! Homecoming game is Friday night at seven, and we Broncos are gonna beat GHS so hard they'll cry."

The girl announcer sighed. "Yes, and then Saturday night the *real* party begins. Make sure to get your tickets early. And, boys, get asking your ladies out so they can get a dress in time!"

"Oh, and remember," the guy announcer grinned wickedly. "No booze." He held up a picture of beer bottles. "No weapons." He held up a picture of a Nerf gun, and some people in class giggled. "And absolutely *no* pets." He grabbed the next picture, and it wasn't an animal at all.

It was Skye.

The picture had been taken in the cafeteria. She had worn a Rainbow Dash getup that day, and she looked like she was growling. Someone must have snapped it on their phone.

The class broke into laughter.

Mr. Rivera hadn't even seen it since he was writing stuff on the board for the upcoming lesson.

My eyes went to Skye. She was watching the screen because her head was turned that way, but I couldn't quite see her expression since she faced forward. Her hand tightened around her pencil until it shook. She put it down.

"Pet?" someone said. "More like wild animal."

More laughter.

"Probably has rabies."

People thought they were so funny, when really they were cruel. They had to know Skye heard them, too. And yet she sat there pretending none of it was happening. I remembered that position well.

Shoulders turned in, hiding, protecting myself against words that could slice deeper than any weapon.

I still carried the scars of words that had cut me, of wounds so deep I was still healing from them. I couldn't deal with that happening to another person right in front of me. I finally snapped. All the anger I'd pent up for years as the weak kid who was too klutzy to play football . . . it all came out right then in a surge of bravery.

I stood up, my fists balled. "It's not funny!"

Everyone went silent, looking at me like I'd lost it. Maybe I had. Even Mr. Rivera stared. "Drew, is there something wrong?"

"Yes." I pointed to the TV, where the announcements were still on. "That jerk held up a picture of Skye when he said no pets at the dance, and everyone thinks it's funny when it's just plain mean."

"Did that really happen, class?" Mr. Rivera looked across the room. No one looked back at him with their guilty faces.

"Of course it happened," Skye said quietly. "Nothing new."

"If you don't like being teased," a guy at the back of the class said, "maybe you should stop showing off that you like a stupid baby show."

"It's not stupid!" Skye and I said at the same time.

Everyone's eyes turned back to me, and I knew my anger had taken me one step too far. Even Skye's eyebrows raised in surprise. But worse, I caught Emma's expression from across the room. Utter betrayal.

"What? Have you watched it or something?" the guy laughed.

I could have said no. Part of me still wanted to, but I thought of Holly and how she said people who like MLP should be loyal to each other. Besides, even if I denied it, people wouldn't stop believing it was true. So I took a deep breath and sealed my fate as the loser guy who liked cute little ponies. "Yeah, I've watched it. All the episodes even. It's a really good show—you could learn a lot about how to be a better person if you gave it a chance."

A few people gasped. Others snickered. I sat down, my face beet red. Nothing else was left to say, and I couldn't take the embarrassment, even if I had brought it on myself. So much for flying under the radar. Skye faced me, but I was even afraid to look at her.

"Is that really true? You like My Little Pony?" she whispered.

The hope in her voice, the lack of judgment . . . convinced me to answer as I anxiously doodled in my notebook. "You did a good job making your Princess Celestia outfit. The colors are spot on."

Mr. Rivera spoke instead of her. "Okay, class, let's get one thing straight. It is *not* okay to bully anyone, and especially over something as small as someone's preferred entertainment. Good media—no matter the intended age group—can be enjoyed by people of all ages. So let's move on to learning about old dead guys who wrote for other old dead guys so that now you, too, can enjoy their works."

No one laughed at Mr. Rivera's joke this time. Maybe it was just me, but class was extremely awkward after that. I *felt* people staring at me, but every time I dared to look up, I didn't catch anyone. The lesson was lost on me since I was preparing for the inevitable.

Word would get out fast. Maybe it already had thanks to stupid cell phones. If I thought Skye got crap for liking MLP . . . I'd get ten times more because I was a guy. I decided to walk on the outer borders of the school to get to my lunch spot instead of through the halls, which always reduced the chances of people finding me. Dad would hear for sure. I wondered how he'd take it, or if he'd even mention it now that we were officially not speaking unless absolutely necessary.

It would be ugly, and yet I wasn't as scared as I had expected to be when my secret got out. Maybe I was in shock. Or maybe it felt like this huge weight was off my shoulders.

The bell rang, and I took my time getting my bag packed. Skye did the same thing. I caught her glancing at me, so I figured I should say it. "Before class . . . I was gonna ask you if you wanted to eat lunch with me so I could tell you that. But I guess you already know now."

Her smile was sad, as if she knew I was about to be in a world of hurt. "Can I eat lunch with you anyway?"

"Yeah, of course." I got up and threw my backpack over my shoulder. "Guess I'll see you later."

"Drew?"

I looked back, and for once Skye didn't look like a prickly cat about to snap. She seemed as gentle hearted as Emma. "Thanks. And sorry."

"Don't worry about it." I left because I wasn't sure what else to say with Mr. Rivera watching. Besides, I would be late for my next class if I didn't hurry.

As I pushed through the halls, I probably should have felt worse. I'd basically ruined the next four years of my life in one move, but all I thought about was lunch with Skye. It'd be the first time in the history of my school years that I'd eat with someone I *wanted* to. And that was kind of awesome.

Chapter 19

WORD SPREAD LIKE a bad cold. By the end of third period, people mocked me and asked if it was true. If I didn't answer, they said I was hiding it. If I did, they asked me if I was gay, or called me a sissy boy, or straight up laughed in my face and called me a freak. I was prepared for this, but it still hurt. The lunch bell ringing, for once, was a relief—it meant I could hide and see Skye, who at least understood.

I'd been sitting at my usual lunch spot in the abandoned art hall for seven minutes when Skye finally showed up and plopped down next to me. She leaned against the wall. She didn't have a lunch tray, and I wondered if she had started skipping lunch at some point. "Sorry I'm late."

"Seems to be your thing," I said.

She laughed. It was the first time I'd heard it, and it made me smile. "It is, actually. Time is hard for me."

"I see." I bit into my sandwich, not sure where to go from here. It felt oddly . . . comfortable, which made it weird. It had never felt this easy to talk to a girl.

"So," she said when the silence had gone on longer than it should. "You're a Brony. Coulda told me that sooner."

I coughed on my food. "A what?"

She raised an eyebrow. "You don't know what a Brony is?"

"No." I took a drink from my water bottle. "I started watching it with my sister a little over a month ago. I haven't told a soul up until today."

"Seriously? You haven't searched the Internet for all the goodies?" She put her hand to her earrings. I hadn't noticed them before. They were in the shape of Princess Celestia's cutie mark. "I bought these from a girl in California who only makes My Little Pony jewelry. She's a Pegasister—that's what girl fans are called sometimes. And guy fans are called Bronies. Or sometimes everyone is called a Brony. It's a little confusing."

It took a moment for me to process this. "Are you saying there are, like, a lot of guys who like this? Not just me?"

She nodded. "A ton! Dude, you need to get online."

"I am . . . kinda." My stomach flipped as I thought of my drawings. Showing them to Holly was one thing, but Skye? She was legit. Hardcore.

"What's that supposed to mean?"

I shrugged. "Never mind. I'll look up Bronies, okay?"

"Good." She cringed a little. "Just . . . be warned there's some super *weird* stuff, too. And some dirty stuff."

My eyes went wide. "Seriously?"

She nodded. "There's so much fan content you could drown in it, and there's a stroke for every folk, you know?"

"Interesting . . . thanks for the warning." I couldn't even begin to imagine what she referred to, but I guessed I'd find out soon. "It's nice to know I'm not actually as alone as I thought I was. I felt like I was crazy for a bit."

"I know." She let out a long sigh—like she knew exactly what I'd gone through—and leaned her head back on the wall. "Hey, so, I'm sorry, but you're gonna get a lot of crap for what you did in English. You probably already have a good idea. Just figured I should warn you in case."

"Yeah, it's already started." I leaned my head back, too. There was something about Skye. It was like I got her even though I hardly knew anything about her. Like being with Quincy—easy to be friends for no reason. "Actually, it's nothing new. My dad only brought me here because I was bullied so bad in middle school. I got made fun of and beat up all the time. Guess it's unavoidable for me."

She looked over at me, her white pony ears making her look like a quizzical cat. "Really? You don't live around here?"

"About an hour away."

"Wow." She grabbed her backpack, pulling some light purple fabric out of it. "Why'd everyone get on your case so bad?"

"Because my dad's a legendary football coach and I suck at football." I watched what Skye was doing. With the fabric came a needle and thread. Finally, she pulled out a hand-sewn patch in the shape of Twilight's cutie mark. "He was hoping to get me playing again, but I told him I hated football and now he's not talking to me."

"So that's why you were sitting with the jocks at first." Skye pinned the patch to the fabric and threaded the needle with purple thread. "Gotta admit that seemed weird."

I laughed a little. "It was. I think my dad made them."

"You know, it reminds me of this one episode . . ." She didn't take her eyes off her work, but I didn't mind. It made it easier since her focus wasn't on me.

"Babs Seed?" I said.

She looked up from her sewing with a bright smile. "Yes!"

"That was the first episode I saw, when I was babysitting my sister. Made me feel like a jerk." I finished off my sandwich. Another reason why it felt so easy was because Skye spoke the same pony language. We had an immediate connection because of this show we both liked. Finally, *finally*, I could reference things I'd absorbed from the show and someone besides Holly would get it.

"That's fantastic. My first episode was—" Her stomach growled so loudly I swore it echoed in the hall. She cringed. "Sorry."

I handed her my bag of chips. "Gave up on the lunch line?"

"Yeah . . . thanks." She opened the bag, hungrily eating a few. "That guy you threatened with the video before? His name's Teagan. Won't leave me alone, and he's gotten even meaner since then. He's in my math class. Must be an idiot if he's a senior taking freshman math."

"Seriously. Too stupid to take a hint."

She smirked. "You know, the guys who are just mean don't bother me so much. But him? He's just plain scary. He says I belong to him even though I've told him I hate him."

"What?" My jaw hung open.

"He says it's destiny or something." She let out a strained laugh, as if she tried to make it not a big deal. "He's basically crazy."

"Are you okay? Have you told anyone?" Maybe I didn't know Skye well, but I was worried about her. Teagan sounded like serious danger, especially from what I'd already seen.

She shrugged. "You know how it is . . . but hey, maybe it'll help now that I'm not alone. I mean, if we keep hanging out."

"Of course we will," I said without hesitation. "We Bronies gotta have each other's backs, right?"

"Right." She smiled and looked less tense than when she was talking about Teagan. I had felt Skye needed a friend, but hadn't realized just how badly she needed one. "So, I know we don't know much about each other, but you gotta come with me to the next Brony meet-up. You'd love it."

I blinked a few times, trying to comprehend the quick change in topic. It still wasn't quite registering. "Okay, what is a Brony meet-up?"

Skye shook her head, smiling like she enjoyed me being such a noob. "Oh, you have no idea the can of worms you opened. Bronies and Pegasisters get together, like, pretty often. From all around the world. We hang out and do pony stuff and just enjoy spending time with other people who get it. There's even BronyCons."

"Cons?" This blew my mind. Were there really that many people who liked MLP? "What the hell are those?"

"Conventions?" Skye crumpled the empty chip bag. "They invite some of the creators of the show, have panels and dances, and people sell pony stuff. I've never been, but it's my dream to go and compete in the cosplay contests."

"I had no idea it was that big." I was both overwhelmed and excited. There was so much I still didn't know, but I had a way to learn and people to do it with. "Where's this meet-up?"

"In Austin. At the community college." She picked up her sewing. "This Friday, actually."

"Really?" It couldn't have been more perfect. That was the Homecoming game. Dad wouldn't drive home until after the game, so I'd be stuck at school that whole time anyway. Judging by the away games I'd already waited through, I'd have until at least ten at night. "Could you give me a ride?"

"Of course! Just meet me in the Home Ec room after school."

"Home Ec room. Got it." After school made me think of Emma . . . of the way she had looked at me in English. I wanted to believe she'd still talk to me, but I felt it wouldn't be that easy.

Chapter 20

SURE ENOUGH, AT the library after school, Emma wasn't at our usual table. For a moment I thought about just doing my homework in peace. If Emma wanted to be childish about it, then whatever. Then I thought about what Twilight would do—she'd never let go of a friend over something like this. And Emma was a friend, just like Skye was becoming my friend, too.

Now if I could get Emma and Skye to be friends with *each other* again. . . .

I walked quietly toward the fantasy section, worried that Emma might hide if she heard me. Peeking around the corner, I expected her to be sitting there like the first day of school. But she wasn't.

I pursed my lips. There's no good reason for her not to be here. She was on the last book of her current fantasy series, and she hated being left on a cliffhanger.

I checked the next row. And the next. I finally noticed her shoes poking out from behind a desk in the far corner. She was hiding, and I felt a bit guilty for hunting her down when she didn't want to be around me. But I didn't want to let Emma go.

Taking a deep breath, I strode over and leaned on the top of the desk. "Are we playing hide and seek now?"

She squeaked and glared coldly at me. "Go away, traitor."

I sighed. "Emma, c'mon."

"Shh, I'm trying to read." She lifted the book higher to block her face.

I squatted down next to her. "Look, I knew you might be this way if you found out, which was one of the many reasons I tried to keep it a secret, but I guess I'm not as good at secret-keeping as you are."

No answer.

"You really won't be friends with me anymore?" I tried again. "Do friends have to like all the same things? I figured real friends could be as different as night and day and still stay friends." *Like Applejack and Rarity.*

Her eyes peeked over the edge of the book, eyebrows knit tight over them. "Go hang out with Skye."

"What if we all hang out together?" I said, angry that she pushed me away after I had made the effort to find her.

She dropped the book. "What?"

"You regret what happened between you and Skye. I think you'd really like the show. So why not just hang out and watch it and be who you want to be?"

She looked at me, shocked. Shaking her head, she said, "Leave me alone. Right now."

"Emma, please. It's doesn't have to be this way." Things were supposed to work out like they did in MLP. I was honest with her, and kind, and all that stuff.

"I know." She pursed her lips, and tears formed in the corner of her eyes. "But I *like* my secrets being secret. If I did what you did, everyone would know. You just went where I'm not ready to go, and I'm jealous and angry and sad right now. So just . . . let me *read*."

Here I thought I knew Emma, but in that moment I realized there was so much more to know. She was as trapped as I was and just as scared to break free. I was slowly getting the courage to escape—she didn't have that yet, and no one could push her out of a box she refused to leave. I saw it all over her face. She wanted to read, pretend none of this was happening, and forget her own problems for a second. I wouldn't take that from her.

I sighed. "Fine. But I'm not giving up on you."

She pouted. "Don't say stuff like that."

I laughed, lightening the mood like Pinkie Pie would have. "Whenever you're done torturing yourself, I'll be at the table doing homework like usual."

As I walked off, I hoped she wouldn't call my bluff and realize how desperate I was to keep her as a friend.

Chapter 21

THE SOUNDS OF sportscasters were familiar to me with the cadence of speech turning into a speedy burst of narration. The voice went higher as players made their moves and the results became clearer. Ironically, Quincy wasn't watching sports—he was watching people play video games.

"See, Mom?" he said as he pointed at the tournament streaming on the TV. "It's a real thing!"

Mrs. Jorgenson had her hands on her hips, staring at the screen. "So these guys are really paid to play this game?"

"Yes!" Quincy stood up and went to the TV, acting like a weathercaster as he pointed out each thing on the screen. "This is the game, and the players are controlling these characters. See their faces down here and how the names above the characters match? And this is the score. . . ."

I only half listened. Quincy didn't need to convince me, and I had other things to investigate. Mainly, the world of Bronies. I was curled into a chair in the corner of the room, figuring I was safe to check out stuff. I could shut down the app the second someone came over.

I typed "Brony" into my phone's browser. It had never occurred to me to search for other MLP fans online until Skye suggested it. I guess I had pictured them all as little girls like Holly, and that would make me a huge creep. But as I stared at the stuff that came up in my search, I didn't know what to think.

There was a whole wiki for the show, plus definitions of what a Brony was. On top of that, I even found a documentary about Bronies. I'd definitely watch that later. There were pictures of guys dressed up in pony gear like Skye, and a crap ton of fan art way better than mine. I found the BronyCon Skye had mentioned—it looked pretty awesome, not that my parents would ever let me go.

I also found the *weird* stuff Skye had referred to, the suggestive pictures and even some gory stuff—so not like the show.

But still, as I went down the rabbit hole of links and images, I didn't feel as alone. I wasn't the only guy who liked this, not by a long shot. From the pictures it seemed like guys from all different walks of life were Bronies. Not just geeks but military guys, too. It was cool to see how far MLP could reach, and it only made me want to be part of it more.

At the same time, a seed of apprehension was planted when I thought about going with Skye to the Brony meet-up. These guys were serious fans—they'd probably know way more than me and think I wasn't one of them because I was so new to this. I'd barely gotten the courage to say I liked the show, and I didn't hold a candle to guys who were such outspoken, proud fans.

Plus, I'd be with Skye. Alone-ish. Was this, like, a date? Suddenly, saying I'd go seemed like a bad idea all around.

"What are you looking at?" Quincy said, jarring me out of my thoughts.

"What? Nothing!" I closed my browser, but Quincy grabbed my phone with lightning speed.

"You keep saying that!" He opened my text messages. "But you're eyes are glued to this thing all the time. Who're you talking to?"

I tried to get it back from him, but he held it high over my head. Quincy was about five inches taller than me, so I could hardly reach it when I jumped. "I'm not talking to anyone!"

"Sh, sh, sh, sh," he ticked as he looked through my messages. I knew that all he saw were texts from him and my mom. He looked back at me when he was done. "Okay, you're not texting a girl. Then what the crap are you looking at on this all the time? And no lying."

I sighed deeply. It was already out at school. Why I had such a hard time telling Quincy, I didn't know. But I snatched my phone from him and tapped on my browser again. I held it out for him to see so I wouldn't have to explain. "There, are you happy?"

He tilted his head, looking at the search results. "Bronies? What the heck is Bronies?"

I rolled my eyes and tapped on the definition link. "This."

He read it. Something must have clicked because his brows popped up and he looked at me. "Hey, this is the thing that Skye girl likes, right?"

I nodded, taking my phone back.

"Did you, like, watch it?"

I nodded again. "With Holly, that night I had to babysit . . . and then, well, I kept watching it."

Quincy stared at me, his face motionless save for a few nostril flares. It felt like forever before he said. "So, you're a Brony. That's what you've been hiding?"

"Yeah, that's the big secret," I said.

"Huh . . ." Quincy pursed his lips, and I knew he wasn't going to take this like I hoped. "I was definitely not expecting that."

"I figured."

"So, you actually like the show?" Quincy wouldn't look at me when he asked.

This put me on the defensive. I had been understanding when he said he wanted to be a pro gamer—which was not at all a normal career—and now here he was judging me about My Little Pony. He was supposed to be my best friend. "Do you have a problem with that?"

"No!" Quincy winced. "Well, it's just a little weird, is all."

"Weird." I'd heard worse at school, but it hurt more coming from someone I hoped had my back. Was this how Skye felt when Emma wouldn't give the show a chance? Was this how they stopped being friends? I didn't want to lose Quincy, but it seemed like a real possibility at this point.

"It's, like, all pink and girly," Quincy continued. This time he looked at me uncomfortably. "You're not . . ."

"No, I'm not gay. That's what you were about to say, right?" I'd heard it so many times at school, but hearing it from him made me want to hit things. "That's so messed up! Gay people can like all sorts of stuff—you're not gay because you like a girl show!"

Quincy held up his hands, his wince tic in full force. "Okay! Sorry, it was just the first thing I thought of."

"I seriously thought you'd be less judgmental. I didn't laugh at you when you said you wanted to be a pro gamer—I just supported you," I said, my anger at the insults boiling over. "You of all people should be open-minded. You know what it's like to be judged."

"What's that supposed to mean?" Quincy glared at me in return. "Are you talking about my tics?"

I didn't say anything, knowing I'd gone too far.

"So just because I'm a freak of nature I am supposed to automatically be this perfect person who understands everyone and everything?" Quincy sh-sh-sh-ed me and punched a pillow. "Gah! Screw you, Drew. Sorry for not being perfect and thinking it's a little weird that you like pink ponies! I was only asking because I was *trying* to understand."

"Whatever." I wanted to leave. This was not how it was supposed to go. "Just forget it. Forget everything. I was going to ask you for advice because Skye asked me to go somewhere with her, but never mind. It couldn't possibly be a date. I'm a sissy boy. I'll get out of your way."

"Drew, wait!" Quincy called as I headed to the door.

I didn't. I left his house, running away because I couldn't face him. Maybe I overreacted, but I didn't know what else to do. I needed him to be okay with it, even if he didn't want to get into MLP like me. But he wasn't. Of all the people who'd judged me, my best friend's opinion hurt the most.

Chapter 22

NOW THAT THE word was out, things kept getting worse at school. In small ways, like how people in class wouldn't partner up with me unless I was the very last person left. In big ways, like how people would ask me if I had mental problems or if I was gay.

"You gonna start dressing up, too, Drew?" a guy said when Skye and I walked out of English together.

"Ooo, kinky!" his friend laughed.

They walked off like it was nothing, just a drive-by "joke" to entertain themselves on the way to class. A few people looked at us, obviously having heard, and giggled.

I wanted to say it didn't bother me, but I'd be lying if I did. Even with Skye there to share in the grief, it still sucked.

Skye rolled her eyes. "I don't see what the big deal is. Cheerleaders wear their costumes, and jocks wear theirs. Why can't I wear mine?"

I shrugged. "I don't know. They're not even costumes—they're clothes. The cosplay stuff I saw online is way more elaborate."

"Right?" She smiled widely. "I'm working on a really cool piece for competition, if I ever save up enough to go to a con, that is. It's going to be epic."

"Yeah? What character?" I liked a lot of things about Skye, but the best one was her drive. She knew what she wanted and she went for it full force. The more I was around her, the more it was rubbing off on me. I wanted to find that thing that made my life have meaning. I had an idea, but I still wasn't 100 percent sure like her.

"That's a secret still. Don't want *anyone* stealing my idea," she said. "But hey, so later on, meet me in the Home Ec room, okay? We can walk to my house after I finish up my sewing for the day."

"Walk?" This shouldn't have thrown me, except that I remembered Emma saying she and Skye lived close to each other.

"Yeah, it's like fifteen minutes. Then my mom will drive us into Austin, okay?" Skye broke off, going down a different hall to class. "See ya!"

I waved, heading towards my math class, my mind stuck on Emma. Something was off. Emma waited after school for her mom to pick her up. Why?—when she could walk home? I'd taken that simple piece of information as fact, but now it seemed like she had been lying to me.

****

A big part of me still dreaded the ringing of the lunch bell. My chest constricted, and my breathing got short and panicky. Even knowing I had Skye to sit with, even knowing we had a good out-of-the-way spot to hide, the memories from middle school haunted me.

So I kept my head down as I headed into the halls. I stuck near the lockers, pushing against the crowds headed for the cafeteria and commons. I went around the back of the school, ending up in the art hall with little risk of threats finding me.

I was almost out of the hall, almost to safety, when a hand came around my arm. My back hit the lockers, and I braced for what usually came next while covering my face for protection.

"Oh, sorry, man," a familiar voice said. "You okay?"

I peeked over my arm, seeing a football jacket over a wide chest. I looked up further at Jake's face staring back at me. "Jake? What're you doing here?"

He looked from side to side. "Can we talk for a second?"

"Uh . . . sure."

"This way." If it had been anyone but Jake, I probably wouldn't have followed him out behind the giant trash bins. Even so, I still partially expected the rest of the football team to appear and beat me up for leaving them and becoming a pony-loving freak. Jake must have sensed this because he said, "Calm down, I'm not gonna hurt you."

I breathed, relieved. "Then what?"

"Look, Drew . . ." Jake put his hands in his pockets. "You're smart. I'm sure you know your dad asked me to help you out as the new kid."

"I figured as much, yeah."

"Well, okay. At first I wasn't on board, but after hanging out with you a bit I decided you're a pretty cool person." Jake looked down embarrassed. No wonder he took me out here where no one would see him being sentimental. "So I just wanted to ask—is it really true you're into that little girl pony show? Or is that a rumor?"

I grabbed the straps of my backpack, a knot in my gut. For a second, it felt like confessing to my father. Just a nicer, younger version of him. "Yeah, I like the show. Is that so bad?"

Jake cringed. "Yeah, it is, actually. It's that bad. At least here, smack dab in the middle of football-loving Texas. You couldn't have kept it a secret at least?"

"I tried. But I couldn't take Skye getting bullied anymore."

"You think you can stop it now?" Jake look concerned for me, and I appreciated that despite his yelling. "You should have stayed with me, told me about it so I could speak up and tell the guys to stop. You can't do anything when you're the target. Trust me, I know. But now? Damn it, Drew, I can't protect you from this without going down with you."

My fists tightened around my backpack straps. "I never asked you to protect me, and I never asked my dad either. And you couldn't have stopped *everyone* from bullying Skye, either."

"Neither can you!" Jake threw his hands up in the air. "Just what are you trying to do anyway?"

"I'm trying to be myself!" I yelled back. Jake's eyes widened, and I imagined I had the same expression since I hadn't known I'd say that either. In that moment I knew it was true. "I'm tired of trying to be what my dad wants, or what everyone else thinks I should be. All that's done is made me miserable. So yeah, I know liking My Little Pony is practically a death wish here, but it's a good show and I like it. And Skye is a nice person I like hanging out with. And I hate getting crap for that, but I don't know what else to do."

Jake sighed, sadder than I expected. "Well, you got balls, Drew. I wish I had the guts to be myself. But don't tell anyone I said that."

"Who would believe me anyway?" I said.

He smirked. "Sadly true."

"So what happens now? We part ways and pretend we never talked?"

"Maybe." Jake looked at the entrance to the hall. "But hey, I'm rooting for you. Even if it doesn't look like it, I am."

"Thanks, I guess." I pointed behind me. "Can I go now? Skye's probably wondering where I went."

"Yeah, see ya."

"See ya." I headed around the school, trying to make sense of why Jake wanted to see me at all. He hadn't offered me any solutions or aid, just a secret vote of support. It reminded me a lot of how I was on Skye's side but hadn't admitted it before I watched the show. She must have felt like this, knowing I wasn't an enemy but not a friend either. It was really confusing.

"There you are!" Skye said, looking me over with concern. "Are you okay? No one gave you crap, did they?"

I shrugged. "Not really. Just had to ask the teacher something."

There was no point in telling her about Jake, in telling anyone about it. It wasn't like his support would change anything if he wanted to keep it to himself. But I was very interested in finding out something from Skye. "So, you said we'd walk to your house, right?"

Skye nodded as she ate from her sad bag of Goldfish crackers. "Yup. Why?"

"It's just . . . don't take this wrong, okay?" I started.

Her eyebrows narrowed. "That's a dubious way to start."

I took a deep breath and tried to frame it in a way that wouldn't give away Emma's secrets. "So, I kinda know Emma Lindsey. She said you guys are neighbors."

Skye choked on her Goldfish, coughing and sputtering. "What?"

"She happened to mention that you guys used to be friends, and—"

"Did she say horrible stuff about me?" Skye groaned. "Why do you have to know her?"

"Calm down." I put my hands out like I was soothing a wild animal. "She didn't say anything bad. That's not even why I brought it up. I stay after school most days because my dad has football, right?"

"Right . . ." Skye settled back down, waiting.

"Well, I run into people while I'm waiting around and one of those people was Emma. She told me that she waits for her mom to pick her up after work, but then you said your house was within walking distance. So I wondered why she wouldn't just walk home. And if she lied, why would she lie about that?"

"Hmm, interesting." Skye settled into the wall, mulling it over. "Well, her parents are crazy overprotective, so maybe she's not allowed to walk home."

"Really?" That wasn't the answer I had hoped for. In my head, I wanted it to be that she stayed to read and hang out with me but was too embarrassed to say it.

"Yeah, like, they're seriously crazy."

I smirked. "This coming from the girl in pony garb."

"Hey!" she sounded mad for a second but then laughed. "Okay, fair enough. But still, they won't let her do *anything*. I used to play there when I was a kid, and they didn't have a TV or computers or even cell phones. They're way strict. Emma would get mad at me when I did stuff she couldn't, and I just couldn't keep living like her when I didn't have to, you know?"

"Yeah, I get that."

It sounded like Skye didn't hate Emma either, which gave me hope that I could eventually get them back together. I just had to create the right opening.

Chapter 23

EVEN THOUGH IT was a long shot, I decided I'd at least see if Emma would bite. So as I entered the library, I pulled up my video streaming app and opened the first episode of My Little Pony. From what Skye had said, Emma never had a chance to watch it with no technology in her house. Maybe if I gave her the chance. . . .

She was hiding behind the desk again, reading her book and not looking up as I stood before her. My heart twisted a little. I wanted her not to be mad at me. Especially after what happened with Quincy, I didn't need my friends hating me over this. I had to fix it.

"Hey." I kneeled down, blocking her book with my phone. "Here."

She glared at the screen and didn't look at me. "Are you trying to tempt me?"

"Maybe," I admitted. "You're surrounded by temptation here anyway."

"Drew . . ." She leaned her head back on the wall, closing her eyes. I felt a twinge of guilt. It looked like she might cry and I didn't want that. "Why do you have to do this to me?"

I pulled back my phone. "Sorry."

She sighed. "I know you don't get it."

"I don't get a lot of things." I almost brought up that she could be walking home right now, but I didn't. She didn't want to tell me these secrets, and I wouldn't force them out of her. "But I wanted to give you the chance to watch it, just in case there was the tiniest bit of desire. You're a writer. I think you'd really appreciate the story."

"Who said I was a writer?" she asked, narrowing her eyes.

"It's obvious, once someone gets to know you." I pursed my lips, holding my phone out to her one more time. "Just take my phone and ear buds. I know you'll love it."

She looked at the phone, and before I knew it she had snatched it from me. "You suck."

I couldn't help smiling as I handed the charger over, too. "I know. Keep it over the weekend. No one calls or texts me anyway."

"Okay." She held it close like something special. But she didn't look at me. "I'm almost done with my book, so . . ."

"Say no more." I went back to my table, hope swelling in my chest. Maybe Emma was still mad at me, but she had taken my phone. Maybe she'd watch the show and realize nothing really divided her and Skye.

I did as much of my homework as I could before I met up again with Skye. She said she'd be sewing for at least an hour and a half, so I might as well work before I play. Besides, I planned to follow Emma and see if her mom really did pick her up. I had to at least know if she was lying, even if I didn't know the reason.

When Emma left the library about forty minutes later, I counted to sixty before I got up and headed for the door. I carefully looked around the corner. Emma was almost to the front entrance of the school. She went through the door as I stepped into the hall. I was pretty sure she wouldn't see me, since I didn't even have to walk outside to confirm my suspicions.

I looked out the glass and spotted Emma in her plaid dress and boots. She wasn't getting into a car— she was crossing the street out front.

So she had lied to me.

It seemed like a stupid thing to lie about. I had no idea what to make of it, but I wasn't as mad as I thought

I'd be. Emma fascinated me. How could she be so open one minute and so closed the next? I decided not to confront her about it because she might start leaving school on time. Which meant I wouldn't get to talk to her at all.

Heading to the Home Ec room, I focused on what was ahead. I was about to go to my first Brony meet-up. I let myself be excited about that, despite the unknowns. There was no way it wouldn't be fun to meet other fans of the show. Plus, I'd get to hang out with Skye.

The sound of the sewing machine echoed through the hall, and this time when I peeked into the classroom I didn't get glares. The teacher smiled and said, "You must be Drew. Skye has told me about you."

I nodded.

Skye stopped sewing and turned around to greet me. "Hey! I'm almost done serging this skirt. It'll take me about fifteen to do the hem and then we'll go, okay?"

"Sure." I sat down in one of the chairs near a big table covered in fabric scraps. The colors were now as familiar as those of Twilight and Fluttershy. There were also pattern pieces made of paper, a measuring tape, and a pair of scissors. "What're you making now?"

"Remember that skirt I was sewing a patch on earlier?" she said as she switched to another sewing machine.

"Yeah."

"Well, that was for an order." She glanced at me shyly. "Actually, I decided to open up an Etsy shop to see if I could sell some clothes. I've sold three things just this week!"

"Really?" I smiled with her. "That's awesome! So you're a real fashion designer now."

She laughed. "No, but it's still cool. Figure I should at least try and make some cash if I'm spending so much time on this. Maybe I can save enough to go to BronyCon, you know?"

"Sounds like a good plan to me." It blew my mind how she was so prepared, taking so much initiative. I would have never thought I could make money on my own at fourteen.

After she finished, we walked to her house in a quiet neighborhood two blocks from the school. As we passed the plantation-style houses, I wanted to ask which one was Emma's. I didn't, knowing that it might not go over well. Skye chatted about people who would be at the meet-up, but it was hard to keep track of who she was talking about when I hadn't met any of them.

"I didn't mention it earlier . . ." Skye bit her lip, looking nervous. "But my big brother is coming with us, too. He's a huge Brony. And, uh, he has Down syndrome, so don't get weirded out by that."

"Oh, no worries," I said, but it caught me a little off guard to know we weren't going alone. "Why would I be weirded out?"

"Some people are." Clearly there was more to that story, but now wasn't the time to ask. With Quincy for a best friend, I'd witnessed plenty of people being "weirded out." Or downright rude.

Skye stepped onto the path of a light blue house with a browning lawn, and I followed her up to the porch. She unlocked the front door, and we stepped into the quiet, cool space. The place was clean and modest, not much furniture and hardly any pictures on the walls. I followed Skye down the hall into a kitchen that looked like it was rarely used.

"You hungry?" Skye said as she opened the fridge.

"Yeah." I sat on a stool in front of the kitchen island. "No one home?"

"Looks like we beat them." She bit into an apple and tossed me one. I caught it. "Sometimes I win because of traffic."

"I see." I looked around, feeling weird about being in her house alone with her.

"I'm gonna bake some fish sticks. Harley loves them." She went to the oven and pressed some buttons. "Do you want any?"

"Sure." I took a bite of the apple. "Harley's your brother?"

She nodded.

"He and your mom work?"

"Yup, my mom's a manager at a grocery store, and Harley is a bagger." She leaned against the counter, much more at ease than me. "Nothing glamorous, but we get by okay."

She never mentioned her dad, so I decided maybe I shouldn't ask about him. "Cool. My mom stays at home, and I have a little sister who's eight."

"The pony fan?"

I nodded. "Too bad I couldn't bring her. She'd probably love this."

Skye laughed. "You should! There's a couple guys who bring their kids. She'd have friends to play with."

"Maybe someday . . ." I gulped, realizing I hadn't told her this yet. "If I ever tell my parents that I like the show."

She paused, her look growing serious. "Wait, they don't know?"

"They don't even know I'm here," I admitted.

"Drew! Are you crazy?" She was madder than I expected. "What if your dad comes looking for you at school? You'll be in so much trouble! *I'll* get in trouble!"

"The Homecoming game is tonight. That's all he cares about."

She put her hands on her hips. "You should at least tell him you're at a friend's house."

"No way!" My heart raced at the thought. It was all around school that I liked MLP, but I hoped it hadn't reached Dad yet. Teachers weren't usually up on student gossip, were they? "He'd be more mad if he found out I like this stuff. You can get me back to school before the game is over, can't you?"

She sighed. "Probably."

"Good, then he'll never know I left." We had to be back by ten. It wouldn't be that hard.

Chapter 24

JUST AS THE fish sticks were done cooking, a car pulled into the driveway. Skye smiled widely as footsteps sounded in the garage. "There they are!"

The door opened, and in came an older version of Skye in nonpony clothes. She had hair shorter than mine and a big, white smile. A guy with a fauxhawk and glasses followed her—he must be Harley. To my surprise, he was about my height but thicker. He saw me right off, and his grin was contagious. "Is this the Brony?"

Skye nodded as she pulled the food from the oven. "This is Drew."

"Awesome!" Harley came over and hugged me. "Nice to meet you, man!"

"You, too." I hugged him back. If everyone at the meet-up was like him, I had nothing to worry about.

He let go, heading for Skye. "Ooh, fish sticks!"

"I'm Skye's mother, by the way," her mom said as she hung her jacket on a hook. "I will be your chauffeur for the evening."

"Mom, whatever, you love going." Skye divided the food onto plates while Harley grabbed the ketchup. "You're almost as big a Pegasister as I am."

"Shh." Her mom glanced at me. "I'm trying to look like a grown-up here."

"Mom likes Rainbow Dash the best," Harley said as he ate his dinner. "You're going to wear Dash ears, right, Mom?"

Ms. Zook sighed. "If you insist."

"Just so you're warned, Drew . . ." Skye pointed to her pony ears, grinning slyly. "Harley makes sure *everyone* is wearing these before we go."

My eyes widened. While I was a fan of the show, I was definitely not a fan of dressing up. I didn't even do that for Halloween anymore, let alone a random day of the week. "Uh, can I get a pass because I'm new?"

"But it's fun!" Harley said. "Everyone does it. You'll feel left out if you don't."

"That's okay." But I appreciated his concern.

Skye shook her head. "It's gonna happen. You may as well give up now."

Ms. Zook and Harley laughed, but not maliciously. It felt like I was part of their family for a moment. They barely knew me, and yet they were at ease. As they joked around and ate, it occurred to me that I'd never seen a family quite like this before. Quincy's was okay, but much quieter. Mine didn't even resemble anything like this . . . like we *loved* each other.

****

I held the Applejack ears in my lap as we rode to Austin Community College for the Brony meet-up. Harley had worn me down this far, saying I didn't have to wear them immediately, but that I should bring them in case I wanted to once we got there. I cringed at the thought of putting them on.

Skye laughed. "No one at school's gonna see you. What's the big deal?"

"Everyone dresses up," Harley said from the front seat. "For reals."

I'd seen the online pictures of guys dressed in pony gear. I knew they weren't lying. But I guess somewhere deep down inside, I still hadn't quite accepted myself as a Brony even though I loved the show. Putting on these ears was like the nail in the coffin. There would be no going back.

Did I want to go back?

"Here we are!" Ms. Zook said as we pulled into Austin Community College. She drove through the parking lot looking for a spot, and when she found one, she stopped the car and everyone got out.

Except for me.

Suddenly, things seemed surreal. Just how did I get to this place where I was at a Brony meet-up with a family who donned pony ears? Even I knew this looked crazy, and yet here I was. None of it made sense, but then again what I was doing before didn't either. I kept waiting for something to click. I had been following Skye hoping I would figure out what I wanted like she had, but I wasn't any closer.

The back door opened, and Skye got back in. She looked puzzled. "Drew? Are you coming?"

"I don't know." I clutched my chest, realizing it was hard to breathe.

"Is something wrong?"

"Wrong?" My laugh was strained. I must have sounded crazy because Skye leaned back. "Lots of things are wrong! I'm about to go to a Brony meet-up like a . . . like a . . ."

"Loser?" Skye asked in a neutral voice.

"Yeah." I leaned back in the seat, forcing myself to take a deeper breath. "Even my best friend thinks this is weird, Skye. He looked at me like he wasn't sure he wanted to hang out with me anymore—and he's a homeschooled, gamer geek with Tourette's! It's not like he's cool either."

Skye snorted. "Okay, sorry, I know that's not supposed to be funny, but damn."

"Seriously." My laugh was short, and then I became quiet. I looked at Skye. Pretty, confident, weird, kind Skye. "How do you do it? How do you take so much shit? How do you know without a single doubt what you want in life? You're fourteen!"

"Fifteen next month," she grinned.

"A whole month older than me. That must be it."

"Drew, let me tell you a secret." She scooted closer, and my heart raced as I caught a whiff of her floral perfume. "'No one can make you feel inferior without your consent.'"

I paused, mulling it over. "I've never thought of it like that before."

"Eleanor Roosevelt was a smart lady." Skye put her hand on my shoulder, patting it twice. "Look, I know this Brony thing is all new to you. And I know it's weird. Trust me, we all know. But it's also fun and funny and cool. If you decide it's too much after tonight, you don't have to come again. I just thought it might help you to meet other guys who like the show."

I nodded slowly. "Sorry for freaking out. I guess I just thought once I admitted I liked the show, I'd have stuff figured out, but I'm still as confused as ever."

"You'll figure it out." She shoved me. "So calm down and—"

Banging sounded on the car roof, followed by Harley's voice. "Hurry up, we are late!"

"You ready?" Skye said, nodding towards the roof. "'Cause he's only gonna get louder."

"Hurry up! Hurry up!"

Skye rolled her eyes. "He's twenty, but sometimes he acts like a kid."

I scoffed, putting on the pony ears. I'd come this far, so I might as well see it through. Maybe this crazy night would give me the answers I needed. Or at least rule out some things. "Why the hell not? Let's do this."

Chapter 25

WE WALKED DOWN a quiet hall in the English building. College students studied or slept, not even looking our way. It was odd. If this had been Yearling High School, every single person would be pointing and laughing. Yet no one here seemed to give a shit.

A door with a giant pink sign on it was in the distance, surrounded by Pinkie Pie's signature yellow and blue balloons. Clearly we would meet in that classroom.

Harley clapped my shoulder. "You can be on my team for the trivia game. I always win."

"He does," Skye said. "He's a freaking genius with pony trivia."

"Not even the Brony president can beat him," Ms. Zook bragged.

"Then I'm definitely on your team," I said. "I've watched a few times but I'm still a total noob."

"I got your back." Harley opened the door for us.

It was everything I expected and nothing I could have imagined all at once. Harley wasn't kidding when he said everyone dressed up. People were in more elaborate costumes than any I'd seen Skye wear, and those not in costumes had Brony T-shirts on. The white board was covered in rectangular papers with numbers on them—must be the trivia game. An assortment of food and drinks were at the back where children and parents mingled. Almost every age group was covered.

"Harley, my man!" a guy in a red Big Mac shirt said. He looked like he was in college, since he had longer hair and a five o'clock shadow. "I was starting to think you weren't coming."

"Wouldn't miss it!" They fist-bumped and hugged. "We brought a new recruit from Skye's school."

"Ah, I see." The guy turned to me, smiling a welcome smile. "I'm Tyler Parr, the president of this fine Brony chapter. And you are?"

"Drew Morris," I said.

"Nice to meet you!" A woman in an immaculate Twilight Sparkle costume came up next to him. "I'm Frankie, Tyler's girlfriend."

Tyler put an arm around her waist. "And the Vice President."

"*And* my hero," Skye said, ogling her outfit. "Holy wow, is this Grand Galloping Gala Twilight?"

Frankie nodded. "It's my show and tell tonight."

"Show and tell?" I said.

Tyler nodded. "We do show and tell so everyone who wants to can share their pony creations. It's fun to share with other fans in person. At least I think so."

"But first we do trivia!" Harley said and pointed to Tyler. "You're never gonna beat me, Prez."

"I've been studying!" Tyler laughed. "Okay, okay, let's get this competition started. Winner gets a special prize this time."

Harley's eyes widened with excitement. "It's mine."

"Alright, everypony! Let's get this meeting started!" Tyler called. Everyone sat at the desks, and he gave out welcomes, announcements, and a rundown of the evening. Basically it was games, eating, and show and tell.

Then the trivia competition began. We divided into three teams, Harley heading one, Tyler another, and a girl in a Fluttershy wig the third. Buzzers were set up and we gathered around the one we were assigned. Some people watched instead of playing. I kind of wished I'd been a spectator because the competition was fierce. People answered the most specific questions in just seconds. I was totally useless.

Harley was epic. He knew how many episodes featured Derpy. He knew the cutie marks of every pony. He referenced the episodes by number and title. He had memorized the songs. I was pretty sure he was the king of the Bronies.

"What is ear-flop then knee-twitch then eye-flutter?" Harley said.

"Correct!" the 'game show host' guy in a black Brony shirt said. "And that is the last question . . . putting Harley's team three thousand points in the lead!"

"Yes!" Harley jumped up and down, and everyone else cheered along with him. There didn't seem to be any sore losers, just people laughing and having a good time.

"Excellent showing, fine sir." Tyler stood up and bowed to Harley. "And now for your prize . . ." He grabbed a large black case from the wall. I'd never seen anything like it before—it probably came up to my waist and was wide, but thinner like a filing folder. "It's hard to give this up when I know how much I could sell it for, but if anyone deserves it, Harley does."

Tyler pulled out a large sheet of paper, and everyone in the room gasped. My jaw dropped as I took in the image—it was Princess Luna, but the style wasn't quite the same as in the show. It was more dramatic, with lots of contrast between light and dark. Luna looked regal and sad and perfect. Finally, my brain processed that Tyler probably had drawn this poster since he had talked about selling it.

Tyler was an artist.

And a pony artist at that.

"For real?" Harley said as he came forward and took the poster reverently.

"Yup." Tyler smiled. "I did it for my illustration class. Don't really have a place to put it in my dorm room."

"Wow, thank you!" Harley turned around, looking our way. "Mom, can we frame it?"

"We have to!" Skye said.

Ms. Zook laughed. "Depends on how much it costs."

"Framing is pricey. Trust me, I know." Tyler clapped his hands together. "Well, that was my show and tell. Who wants to go next?"

Unlike a normal classroom, people eagerly raised their hands. My thoughts went immediately to the sketchbook in my backpack, but after what Tyler had shown, it seemed dumb to share my little drawings. I wasn't like him—he was obviously studying to be an illustrator or something in college.

But at the same time, as people shared their costumes, stories, pictures, and handmade pony toys, I kept glancing over at Tyler. The artist.

He wasn't some pompous old guy. He wasn't all deep and painting stuff that went in museums. Maybe he did sometimes, but that awesome Princess Luna was also in the mix. He made it *for a class.* Classes where he was allowed to draw ponies. He was freaking in college and drawing cartoons.

My brain was about to explode. Somewhere in the back of my mind I knew people did that, but at the same time I never thought *I* could be one of those people.

But now . . . *now* . . .

A little boy, maybe around Holly's age, went up next with his own colored picture of Rainbow Dash. "This is my best Dash! And I didn't get any help drawing it."

People clapped and cheered and told him it was great, just like they'd complimented everyone who had gone before. I'd seriously never met people who were this nice, this supportive. Maybe I was high on Brony love or something, but I wanted to share my own drawings, too. I wanted to hear them say I was doing a good job. Because a little voice inside of me whispered that maybe I did know what I wanted to do with my life, but no one ever told me it was something I was allowed to do.

"Me next!" Skye said as she stood up. She twirled once so everyone could see her outfit. "I finished this Celestia outfit just last week. I really like how the dress came out, and since it's simple to make, I'm thinking of adding it to my Etsy store if anyone's interested. I'm starting to get orders. It's really exciting!"

"Awesome! Good for you, Skye!" Frankie cheered. "Really great job on the sewing."

"Oh my gosh, thank you!" Skye blushed. She clearly idolized Frankie. Turned out Frankie was Skye's role model—she was a cosplayer who had won dozens of awards at conferences for her My Little Pony cosplays. The outfit Frankie modeled today was her next big thing. It looked spectacular, but she said it wasn't even finished yet.

After Skye sat down, I almost went, but at the last second I chickened out. I almost went again after the guy who read his story about the Cutie Mark Crusaders finally getting their cutie marks. People kept going, and I kept almost going.

It was weird how I wanted to but was terrified at the same time.

Tyler stood up after nearly the whole room had shared. "Okay, is that everyone? Last call!"

I was about to let it go, but Tyler stood up there. I didn't know him at all, but I thought he was cool. He was someone who, for the first time since I had given up trying to be my dad, I wanted to be like.

So I raised my hand.

"Drew, our new friend! What do you have for us?" Tyler motioned for me to come up.

I took a deep breath and pulled out my sketchbook. As I stood up there, I noticed Skye smiling at me, amused. Like a "See? I told you so."

"I'm not that good yet, but I've been drawing a lot because of the show. It's fun. I think I really like doing it."

"That's great!" Tyler said, and my stomach turned over his excitement. "Show us something."

I flipped through my sketches, trying to decide. I ended up on the Princess Cadance and Shining Armor I had done for Holly. "I drew this for my sister. Cadance is her favorite."

I was surprised so many people said positive things all at once. A "Nice!" there. A "Sweet!" there. Harley stood, clapped, and called out, "Hey, you're really good at that!"

"Thanks, guys," I said, feeling my own face redden like Skye's had.

"He's right, you know." Tyler came closer and took my sketchbook. "May I?"

"Sure . . ." I gulped down my nerves as he paged through. This was not in the plan—I was only going to show one picture. Now the real artist looked at my stuff. The mess ups, the good, the clumsy.

Tyler smiled widely as he handed my stuff back. "How long have you been drawing?"

"Not much until a couple months ago."

He raised an eyebrow. "Seriously? You should keep going, dude. You have a lot of potential."

"Really?" I could hardly believe it. This guy was actually good, and he told me I could do what he did? I didn't expect that at all, and it felt beyond awesome.

"Yeah, really. Now, more games!" Tyler laughed, having moved on, not realizing he'd changed everything for me in that moment.

I sat down next to Skye, my mind spinning with excitement.

She leaned over, a big grin on her face. "Why didn't you tell me you were drawing ponies?"

I shrugged, distracted with my own thoughts.

That thing I'd been waiting to happen? I was pretty sure it just had. All the pieces clicked, and a fire lit inside me. My future wasn't this mushy thing I had no idea what to do with. Something was there. Something I knew I wanted, and I finally had the courage to admit it.

I would be an artist.

Chapter 26

I COULDN'T REMEMBER a time I had been this happy. As Skye said, the meet-up and everyone there would be considered freakish by normal-people standards, but as we played My Little Pony Monopoly, listened to songs from the show, and ate cupcakes and drank punch, I had so much fun I felt bad for everyone who didn't get it.

Because this Brony thing was awesome.

For once in my life I understood how it felt to belong somewhere, to be around people who took me as I was and didn't expect me to fit in the molds I tried so hard to cram myself into. Those molds were too small for what I wanted to be; now I felt free and also a little bit invincible.

"Oh, you *have* to get to a con," Frankie said to Skye as we cleaned up the Monopoly pieces. "It's a blast, and people need to see your talent!"

Skye sighed wistfully. "I want to *so* bad, but it's expensive! There's the travel, and the tickets, and the food costs, not to mention the fabric to make my piece."

Frankie nodded. "It is pricey. It's gotten easier for me and Tyler now that we're making a bit of cash from our work. I actually just got a commission for a major Rarity piece, super detailed, competition level—that's going to almost pay for BronyCon."

"You're so lucky." Skye frowned as she glanced over at her mom and brother chatting with another family by the remaining cupcakes. "We don't have the cash for that kind of trip. My mom says I can go . . . if I can earn the money on my own. At the rate I'm selling, it'll take me three years."

"Are the cons like this?" I asked. It was hard to picture something more awesome than the meet-up, but they made it sound like BronyCon was way better.

"Imagine thousands of people all geeking out like this," Frankie said. "Plus they usually invite artists and writers for the MLP franchise, from the show, movies, comics . . . it's so cool to listen to them talk about the show. And then there's the vendor floor where people sell pony stuff. It's fantastic."

"Wow." Although I still couldn't quite picture it, the *idea* of it was enough for me to wish I could go. But there was no way; my parents didn't even know I liked the show.

Skye whimpered, "I wanna go so bad! Forget Disneyland! BronyCon is my dream."

Frankie laughed. "As it should be."

"Hey, everypony!" Tyler called over the chatter. "Here's the sign-ups for food and activities next month. I can't make these parties awesome without you, so get volunteering."

"I'm writing the trivia next time!" Harley called out.

A few people raced to beat him to it, a girl about his age saying, "No one will know the answers if you do it! Let us try and stump you, okay?"

Harley smiled. "Oh, fine."

"Are you signing up, Drew?" Skye nudged me. "Or are you not coming anymore?"

"What? Why wouldn't you come again?" Frankie looked concerned. "Did we do something that made you feel bad?"

I put my hands up. "No! It was fun!"

"He was just nervous before," Skye said. "So? I think we should sign up for food. I saw a fun recipe online for a rainbow cake I want to try. We could make it together after school since you're always stuck there late anyway."

I had to play it cool. So we'd be alone in her house more. No big deal. Maybe. "Sure, sounds good."

"I'll sign us up then." She skipped off, leaving me there with Frankie. Who smiled weirdly at me.

"You two are cute together," she said.

My eyes widened. "What?"

"I'm really glad you go to school with her. She's told me how bad it's been." Frankie patted my shoulder. "She's needed a friend. Good for you for seeing how awesome she is."

It wasn't that hard. That's what I wanted to say, but I worried she might tell Skye. Instead, I watched Skye as she signed up. I definitely liked her, but I still wasn't sure how much of that was being attracted to her and how much was wanting to be like her. Plus, there was still Emma, and I couldn't help thinking that if she were here, all of this would be perfect.

And then I noticed the clock on the wall.

The one that said fifteen minutes to ten. I swore. "Skye! I need to go!"

She looked at me, confused. I pointed to the clock. She saw it and jumped. "Oh no! Mom, we gotta get Drew back to the school like right now!"

"What?" Ms. Zook looked confused as we both descended on her.

Skye cringed. "Drew's parents don't exactly know he's here. They think he's at the school waiting for the Homecoming game to end."

Ms. Zook's jaw dropped and she sputtered, "You have *got* to be kidding me."

I shook my head. "My dad would kill me if he knew I liked this stuff."

"Well, we better hurry then. Don't want your murder on my hands." She did not look happy, but she couldn't do anything about it. "Harley! Let's move!"

"I don't wanna go!" he said with a hint of a tantrum.

"Buddy, please." Skye put her hands together, begging.

Tyler stepped in, putting an arm around Harley. "I'll take him home when we're done, Ms. Zook. You go."

She breathed a sigh of relief. "Thank you so much."

We were out the door and running for the car. It took at least twenty minutes to get to Yearling High from here, which would put us in at just after ten. I told myself it would be okay. There was always over-time, time-outs, and stuff like that to make football games last forever. The fourth quarter alone could be as long as the other three combined.

"Next time . . ." Ms. Zook said through her teeth. "I'm gonna make sure your parents know where you are, Drew. I don't want to be accused of kidnapping or something."

"Yes, ma'am," I said, although I had no intention of telling them. I could take the bus if I had to.

When we pulled up to the school, not as many cars were in the parking lot as I'd hoped. My stomach turned. The game must be over, but the field lights were still on. The lot should be packed, everyone waiting and watching the final plays.

"Drew . . ." Skye said. "I have a feeling you better start saying some prayers."

I sunk in my seat. "It might be okay. The players have to clean up after."

Her mom shook her head as she pulled into the spot nearest the school. "Good luck with that."

"I'll come with you," Skye said.

"I'll wait here," Ms. Zook said.

We got out of the car, and I went to the door nearest the football field. That one would probably be unlocked. Sure enough, it was, but when we stepped inside it was quiet. No raucous sounds coming from the locker room. No one even around except for us.

"I'm so screwed," I said under my breath as we walked down the hall.

"You should call him," Skye said. "Yelling is less bad on the phone."

"I don't have my phone, I gave it to . . ." I cringed, thinking of Emma getting calls from my parents and knowing how Skye would react if she found out I was friends with her ex-best friend.

"Who did you give it to?" Skye pressed. "And why?"

"Drew!" a familiar voice came from the adjacent hall. I looked, and my stomach hit the floor. Emma ran up to me, only glancing at Skye. "Where have you been? Your dad called your phone like ten times, and then I had to answer because he couldn't find you!"

"You gave your phone to *her*?" Skye asked incredulously. "Why?"

"So she could watch My Little Pony," I admitted. "And I was at a Brony meet-up, Emma."

"A what?" Emma shook her head and held up my phone. "Well, your dad and a bunch of his players are scouring the school for you. I was helping since I had no clue where you were either, but my parents are waiting for me in the car. I told them I forgot something in my locker."

I didn't take the phone from her. "Sorry, I should have told you—I thought I could get back in time."

Emma looked behind her to make sure we were alone. "He's *really* mad. It was scary."

I nodded. I felt like I was about to meet the grim reaper, and there was no way around it. "You guys go, okay? If I survive this, I guess I'll see you on Monday."

The girls looked at each other. Skye didn't seem happy about any of this, but she held out her phone to me. "At least give me your number so I can text and make sure you're okay."

"You're assuming I'll be allowed to text." I nodded towards Emma. "Hey, Emma, just keep my phone, okay? You may as well use it while I'm grounded for forever."

"Thanks," she said, holding it to her chest. "He went to look in the auditorium, so he's probably still around there."

"Okay." I put my hands in my pockets, not sure what to do now that I had Skye and Emma in the same place at the same time. Maybe my life was about to get worse, but here was a chance for them to talk at least. "Get home safe. I'll see you later."

I turned, because if I didn't, they'd see how terrified I was to face my father. But as I headed towards the auditorium, I thought about the night I had just experienced and the people I had met. I held onto the happiness and told myself to fight for that no matter what Dad threw at me.

Because I wanted to be an artist.

I *wanted* something for the first time in ages.

I didn't have to enter the auditorium to find my dad. He sat outside on the stairs, talking on the phone to someone. I recognized the guy next to him—Jake. He spotted me first and tapped Dad on the shoulder. He turned, rage in his eyes.

"Found him. We'll be on our way home after I cuss him out," he said to who I assumed was Mom. Then he hung up. "Thanks for helping, Jake. Tell the other boys to get home."

"Yes, sir." Jake glanced sympathetically at me and was off in the other direction.

"Where the hell have you been?" Dad's voice burst out, echoing in the empty hall. "Your mother was about to call the cops and report you missing!"

I looked at the ground, my heart pounding in my chest. I could lie now, say I fell asleep somewhere in the school, but it would only put off the inevitable. I wasn't about to stop watching or liking MLP, and after tonight I cared a little bit less about what other people thought of that. "I went to a Brony meet-up with a friend."

There was a long pause. "You left the school and went where?"

"To a Brony meet-up. Bronies are guys and older people who like My Little Pony," I explained. "I like the show and wanted to meet other guys who did, too."

"What?" Dad's voice went high. He had a hand on his forehead like he was in shock. "That was just a stupid rumor around the school, that you liked that girly show. That wasn't real. My son wouldn't like something like that."

"It's not a rumor, Dad. It's true. It's a good show."
I wished he'd not talk to me like he always did, but as horror filled his eyes, I knew that the stuff he didn't talk to me about was about to spill out of his mouth.

Chapter 27

DAD LOOKED AT me like I was more alien than ever. I was tired. I wanted to go home and sleep now that I had said what I had been so afraid to admit. Turned out it wasn't so bad. I felt liberated, almost, even with Dad about to lay into me.

"So, let me get this straight," he started. "I go out of my way to transfer you here so you can have a clean start, and you go telling people you like a girly cartoon? Do you enjoy being bullied, Son?"

I sighed. "I didn't start telling people—I stood up for my friend who was getting bullied like I was before."

He scoffed. "The one you left school with today?"

"Yeah."

"Why didn't you answer your phone? Too ashamed?"

I narrowed my eyes, angry and on the verge of retaliating. "No. I let another friend borrow it. Notice how I keep using the word 'friend.' I've still managed to make those, even if they happen to be people your dumb ball players make fun of."

"Watch it, boy." He pointed at me. "You're in no position to be giving me lip. You left without permission. You've been lying to us about what you've been doing. And here I find out it's not even to do normal teenager things! You're hanging out with a bunch of freaks and losers!"

"They're not losers!" I yelled back. "I'm not a loser! Just because I'm different than you doesn't make me a freak."

He lost it then, coming right up into my face, his voice full blast. "You are a freak! You're a teen boy watching a show for little girls, which makes you either a pervert or gay."

"WHAT?" I said, trying to match his volume and failing. Stupid coach vocal chords of his. "Are you insane?"

"You're not watching that show again," he growled.

"Are you gonna stop Holly, too, then?" I stepped back from him, worried he might be so mad he'd hit me. "We watch it together—that's why we're getting along better. It's well written, and the animation is good quality, and it doesn't matter if it was made for girls or boys!"

"Holly *is a girl.* Or are you a girl, too?"

I wanted to punch something. Which was a bad idea because I'd probably be the one to get hurt. "So if Holly started watching Ninja Turtles or something, would you freak out like this and tell her she's a lesbian and a pervert for watching a 'boy show'?"

"That's not the same thing!"

"It is!" I folded my arms, containing my anger. "Such a shit double standard."

Dad balled his fists, and I braced myself. But the hit never came. "You're grounded. And you're never going to those freak meetings again. And you will stay in my office after school or on the bench during a game for the rest of the damn year."

"I will not!" I said, the punishment searing my heart because he was taking away all the good things in my life. "It doesn't even affect you! Why can't I just do what I like without you being such a jerk about it?"

"It doesn't affect me?" Dad put his hand on his chest, having the gall to look like he was the victim here. "I can barely tell other people I *have* a son when I think about explaining you to them."

I didn't want his words to cut, but they did. And deep. "You're that ashamed of me?"

"Of course I am! How did I get such a pansy, loser freak for a son?" He looked away, and in that one motion I knew he'd rather I not existed at all. I was that pathetic and shameful to him—a disappointment.

But instead of feeling the usual, awful pang of guilt, something inside of me let it go. I would never be what he wanted. No matter what I did, I wasn't the son he had imagined. That wasn't my fault.

It. Was. Not. My. Fault.

"How did I get such an asshole for a father?" I said under my breath, but it was still loud enough for him to hear.

He shoved me hard enough that I almost hit the ground. "You think you can call your father that? You think you can run off and do whatever stupid thing you want? Fine, find your own damn way home. You ain't gettin' in my truck until you show some respect."

"Good," I said back. I didn't want to sit next to him in his dumb truck anyway.

He stalked off, leaving me alone in the hall. I didn't go after him. I hoped he'd leave me there. Not that I knew what to do after that, but I couldn't stand to be around him after how he had just treated me. I took a seat on the stairs in front of the auditorium, feeling shaky and way too close to crying. I wouldn't cry—if I did, Dad would win. He'd be happy his weak baby son was bawling because of him.

I shoved my palms into my eyes. "Do. Not. Cry."

I didn't have many options. First off, I didn't have my phone, so it wasn't like I could call Mom and ask her to drive all the way out to get me. Who knew whose side she was on anyway? Maybe Dad wouldn't even let her if she tried.

A bus would get me about forty minutes walking distance from my place, except I didn't have any cash.

Skye's house wasn't far, but it seemed pretty awful to show up and beg for help after I had put them out by not telling my parents where I would be. Her mom seemed pretty mad.

I guess I could stay at the school.

All weekend.

"Hey," a voice said.

I jumped, looking up at the last person I expected. "Jake?"

"C'mon, I'll take you home." He started walking, assuming I'd come with him.

"You're not doing this for my dad, are you?" I asked.

He stopped and turned back with a nasty glare. "I'm doin' this for you, idiot. Your dad would bench me for being soft if he found out, so you better keep your mouth shut."

I stood up, still surprised that Jake would do this for me, but I wasn't about to turn down the offer. There was no other way I'd get home tonight, so I caught up and followed him to an old pickup with chipped gray paint. We got in without speaking, and it took him a few times revving the engine to get it started.

"She don't look like much, but she'll get you home. Promise," Jake said, pulling out of the parking spot.

"Thanks." I wasn't going to push when he was saving my ass, but I had to ask, "Why are you doing this again?"

"Because, Drew . . ." He sighed. "You were right, okay? Your dad's kind of an asshole. And I can't believe he'd leave his own kid stranded just because he found out you watch My Little Pony."

"Oh." I kept forgetting that Jake was a decent guy, despite his not showing it to most people.

He gulped, pulling at his collar. "And . . . I mighta watched a couple episodes."

I turned to him, shocked. "What?"

"Just, like, four. To see what all the hoopla was about."

"Seriously?" A giant smile broke out on my face. Freaking Jake Harvey, bulky ball player and tough guy, watched MLP. "And?"

"I guess I can see why you like it, but if you tell anyone that, I'll kill you."

I laughed, this tiny revelation erasing my dad's cruel words for the moment. "That is awesome. And of course I won't tell anyone. You better watch out, though, it's addictive."

He smirked. "It's all your fault."

"Sorry."

And then he spilled his guts to me. "I've worked so hard not to be the loser fat kid I used to be. I learned how to play football. I lost the weight. I stopped playing card games with my nerdy friends, forced myself to go to cool-people parties, found a girlfriend. But you show up and start doing shit like you don't care what people think, and I wonder what the hell I did all this for. I'm not happy. Sometimes I wish I was still that fat kid. I miss my old friends. I miss doing things I like."

It sounded so painfully familiar, like Jake was who I would have been if I'd tried out for freshman football and pretended things were fine. "I thought about trying to do all that, but it felt like too much work."

"It's so much work lying to yourself." He turned on the radio, embarrassed. "Sorry, I'll shut up now."

"Don't worry about it," I said, my mind going to Quincy. "I don't mind. Talking like this, it reminds me of how me and my best friend used to talk. But then I admitted I was into My Little Pony and he kinda made fun of me. It hurt. I was hoping it wouldn't be like that with him, of all people, but it was. Then here you're cool with it when I thought you wouldn't be."

"You make me wish I had a kid brother," Jake said. "We should just pretend."

"Sure." I pointed to the freeway that would get me home. "Take that one."

"Okay."

We didn't say much after that, but it wasn't the cold silence Dad constantly gave me. It was late, and Jake was tired after playing in the Homecoming game. I didn't want to bother him too much more, not when I owed him a ton for picking up the broken pieces of tonight and putting them back together.

Every time things got worse with Dad or school, at least one person out there would be decent. That made this whole "being myself" thing doable.

Chapter 28

I WASN'T SURE what to expect when Jake pulled into my driveway after eleven o'clock. Dad was home, and Mom must have noticed he'd come home without me. Either she'd be mad at him for leaving me or mad at me for disappearing. Maybe both. Probably both.

"I didn't realize Coach lived so far away," Jake said as he looked at our house. "Lots of land."

"Yeah, and we don't even use it." I opened the car door. "Hey, thanks again."

"Don't mention it." He leaned closer, smiling. "No, really, do not mention it ever."

"Got it." I almost told him to be himself since he was way cooler like this than the personality-less football player. But I got out and headed for my house. I had learned by now that people could not be convinced to be themselves—they had to choose it on their own.

I walked slowly, letting Jake back out of the driveway before I got to the house so I would hear if anything was going on inside.

Silence.

But a light was still on.

Pulling out my house key, I unlocked the door and stepped inside. I spotted Mom in the living room, and before I even shut the door, she was on her way to me. She grabbed me by the shoulders and looked me over like I might be injured. "What happened? Where did you go? How did you get home?"

"Dad didn't tell you anything?" I said.

She shook her head, tearing up. "He said you went missing, then he found you. Then he showed up without you and went to bed refusing to explain. What in the world happened tonight, Andrew?"

Andrew. My full name meant she was much more upset than she let on. "He found out I like My Little Pony."

"What?" She hadn't let go of me yet, and her nails dug into my arms. "You mean the show Holly watches?"

I nodded slowly. This conversation was exhausting. How many times would I have to explain this? "I like it a lot, and I started drawing the ponies for me and then for Holly, too. That's why she asked for those colored pencils. Then I found a friend who likes it at school. I went with her to a meeting for other people who are fans of the show. And I met this cool guy who's an illustrator and I think I want to do that. I want to go into animation, but I didn't get a chance to tell Dad that because he freaked over the ponies and told me how ashamed he is of me and how I'm a huge loser."

Mom stepped back but watched me as she processed the information. I couldn't read her expression, and I was too tired to care about which way she'd go at this point.

"You want to be an animator?" she finally asked.

"I think so." It was odd to think I'd only figured it out tonight. It felt like something I had always wanted.

"You've never said you wanted to be anything. Not since football went sour."

"I know."

"But you have a dream now? Because of this show?"

"I guess." I hadn't thought of it that way, that wanting to be an animator was a dream. It was something I realized I wanted to *do*. "The illustrator at the meet-up, his name was Tyler. He's in college for it. He said my drawings were good and I should keep going."

"Really?" Mom smiled. She also cried. I had no idea what was happening. Then she hugged me. "Oh, Drew, that's so great!"

"It is?" I needed to give up predicting how people would react because minus my dad, I had been wrong almost every time.

"Yes! I was always terrified you'd never find what was right for *you* with how your father . . ." Her grip on me loosened. "Oh lord, did he really say he was ashamed of you?"

"Yeah." My voice cracked. Stupid emotions. "He wouldn't even drive me home because I stuck up for myself and told him he was being a jerk."

"I'll talk to him, sugar." She patted my back. "You don't worry about this anymore. It's his problem. He's a proud man and it's annoying as hell."

"Thanks, Mom." After such a long day filled with so many crazy new things, all I could do was hug my mother and not let my tears show. Because not having to deal with my dad? That was what I needed right now.

Chapter 29

ONE THING I never expected to do: willingly go to the guidance counselor. But by Monday morning, when Mom drove me all the way to Yearling High, since Dad wouldn't, I was determined to see Miss Overly. Mom at least supported my decision.

"Andrew Morris?" Miss Overly called when she stepped out of her office.

Mom and I stood up. Miss Overly guided us into her small space, and we sat in the chairs in front of her cluttered desk. The walls were covered with inspirational posters and college brochures, and for a second I got nervous. This was my first real step towards "doing something with my life."

"So what can I help you with today?" Miss Overly asked as she clasped her hands and leaned forward.

"Nothing too serious," Mom said for me. "Just some class changes for next semester."

"Oh?" Miss Overly smiled. "What are we thinking, Andrew?"

"Um, it's Drew," I said and gulped. "I want to take an art class instead of wood shop."

"I see . . ." She typed into her computer. "We can probably work that out for you. Any reason for the change?"

"I'm just thinking about being an artist." The heat rose to my face. I remembered how she had told Skye to have a backup plan. Maybe she wouldn't think it was as great as my mom did. "Figured it'd be good to be in art classes."

"Very true," she said. "What kind of art are you interested in?"

"Mostly cartoons and animation."

She nodded, still looking at her screen. "Those are competitive fields, but there are more jobs there than other artistic focuses. So, because you haven't taken any art classes, you don't have too many options. Basically it's Drawing I or Beginning Arts. All the higher courses require you to have taken those first."

"What's the difference?" Mom asked.

"Drawing I is focused on paper and pencil drawing, I think. It says 'dry media.'" Miss Overly grinned sheepishly. "I don't actually know what that means. The description for Beginning Arts says it covers all art media and forms, so I'm assuming it's not just drawing but painting and sculpting, too."

I pursed my lips, thinking. They both sounded interesting. "You said I need them both to do the higher level classes?"

"Yes, Drawing II, Painting I and II, Figure Studies . . . and if you are good at them, there are Honors and AP classes, but those are by invitation of the art teacher only," she said. "So which are you thinking of?"

"Can I take both?"

Her eyebrows popped up. "Well, your other elective next semester is PE. You need at least two semesters of physical education classes to graduate, so I would recommend not putting that off."

"I'd like to take both if I can." Forget PE. If I got those two classes done, I could get to the cooler ones faster. They'd probably be more work, so I would only do one a semester. I could do PE then.

Miss Overly looked at Mom. "Is that okay with you?"

"Of course. If this is what he wants to do and he can do it, by all means let him." Mom smiled as she looked at me. "He's got a talent for it."

"Okay then, let's move this schedule around." Miss Overly started changing almost my entire schedule. To get in both art classes, I'd have to transfer into different periods for history and math. I was okay with that even if it'd be weird to switch teachers in the middle of the year. It took almost half of first period to work it out, but as I walked out of her office with my new schedule, I could hardly wait for next semester. Too bad it was still six weeks away.

"You look happy," Mom said.

I smiled. "You know, I am. For the most part."

"It looks good on you, sugar." She gave me a side hug. "You run along to class. I'm gonna go shopping in Austin while you're learning. May as well since I had to drive all the way here."

"What about Holly?" I asked. We wouldn't get home in time to pick her up from school. All the details of my transportation had yet to be worked out.

"Quincy's mom is grabbing her for me today."

"Ah." Quincy's mom. Quincy. It felt like ages since I'd seen them. Friday night had been the first time I missed pizza night in a long time, and it happened to be the night my whole life had changed.

"Run along—you're already very late," Mom said. "It'll all work itself out. You wait and see."

"I hope so." I waved and headed down the deserted hall to English. My nerves grew with each step, since it'd be the first time I would see Skye and Emma since Dad yelled at me. I had no idea what to expect, but I figured they'd both have a lot of questions for me.

"Drew, welcome to class!" Mr. Rivera said as I came in. "Just so you know, there's a difference between fashionably late and just plain epically late."

"Sorry." I held up the pink slip Miss Overly gave me. "Was meeting with the guidance counselor."

"Ah." He held out his hand, and I walked to the front to give him the note. "Well, I guess I can't make fun of you now. Way to take the wind out of my sails."

"There's *plenty* you can still make fun of him for," someone nearby mumbled.

I forced myself to ignore the comment and took my seat. Skye was right in front of me, sporting a DJ Pon-3 look. She smacked my arm. "When you didn't show up this morning, I thought you were dead!"

"I am. Kinda," I whispered to her. "At least to my father."

Her eyes widened. "Shit, did you tell him?"

I nodded. "He left me at the school; he was so mad."

"No way!"

Mr. Rivera cleared his throat. "Drew, c'mon. You just got here and now you're flirting instead of trying to catch up?"

The class laughed. I went beet red. "Sorry, sir."

"Fill me in later, I guess." Skye turned back around, a bit embarrassed herself.

I tried to listen to the lesson and take notes, but it only took a minute for me to catch Emma looking at me from across the room. Something in her expression made my heart flip. Not that it was romantic, but I could tell she *wanted* to talk to me. I had missed talking to her so much. Now I had to wait the whole day for it to happen.

Chapter 30

SKYE MET UP with me after school. I'd told her everything at lunch, and she in turn recounted how it had
gone down with Emma after I left to find my dad. They
had kind of talked and I *think* they had figured out that
maybe they didn't have to hate each other. At least that's
why I thought Skye was doing this favor for me.

"My mom should be here soon in a black van," I
said. "Just introduce yourself, keep her busy while I get
my phone from Emma."

"Sure." Skye looked at me slyly. "Go get your phone
from your girlfriend."

My eyes widened. "Don't say that! She's not
my—my—"

"Oh my gosh! Look at you!" She laughed. Hard.
"And here I thought Emma freaked out when I asked
if you were her boyfriend. Your reaction is ever better!"

"Why are you even asking that?" I shoved her
lightly. "She won't even acknowledge me in public.

She'd never . . ." I realized how sad and hurt that made me feel. "You know how she is."

Skye pouted. "Sorry, Drew. I'll shut up."

"Good. We still need her to let go of the 'media is evil' concept. One thing at a time."

"She's almost there. Don't know how you did it, honestly."

I shrugged. "I'll be right back."

"I'm gonna go meet your mom!" Skye waved and bounced off.

I took a deep breath, suddenly nervous to see Emma thanks to all the relationship talk. But I headed for the library anyway. To my surprise, I didn't have to go to the back corner where she'd hidden before. Emma sat at our usual table, a book in hand and my phone in front of her. I walked over slowly, savoring the feeling of seeing her there.

"Hey," I said as I sat in my usual chair.

Emma jumped a little, looking at me. "Hi."

"You watch the show?" I asked, reaching out for my phone and charger.

She nodded, setting down her book. "To episode ten, but I couldn't sneak in more."

"And?"

"It's really cute," she said. "The writing . . . You were right—it's really good. Not that I know a lot about TV show writing, but it flows really well and the characters are strong and unique."

I let out a small laugh. "You sound like a reviewer!"

"What am I supposed to sound like?" She folded her arms, tipping her chin up. "I watched it, and now you're making fun of me for it."

"I am not! I think it's awesome you thought about it that much." I turned on my phone and was surprised to see about forty texts. Half of them were from Quincy, of all people. I figured he thought I was too weird to talk to ever again. And after I was so mean to him, I wasn't sure I even deserved to be his friend anymore. "So will you watch more and hang out with me and Skye now?"

Her eyes narrowed, but she smiled. "I'm thinking about it. But I have other friends, too, you know."

"Bring them along. Friendship is magic and stuff."

I was happy to hear her laugh. But then she became still. "So, how did things go with your dad?"

"A little bit worse than I expected," I admitted. "I think he's kind of disowned me?"

Her shoulders slumped. "That's not encouraging me to come clean to my parents."

"I didn't know that's what I was supposed to be doing!" I put my phone down, scrambling to make up for what I had just said. "My mom was really great though! I told her about how My Little Pony helped me realize I want to be an artist, and she was all over it. That's why I was late this morning—we were with the school counselor changing my schedule to have art classes next semester."

"Really?" Emma said hopefully.

I nodded. "It's been pretty unpredictable how people react to it all. People I thought would be cool with it weren't, others I thought would mock me didn't, and some I guessed right. But overall, I'm happy, Emma. Like, actually happy, despite the hate."

"I'm glad you're happy. And you wanna be an artist?"

"Yeah. Let me show you." I pulled out my sketchbook and gave it to her. It was getting easier to show people my drawings. Maybe because every time I did, people complimented me. And compliments were as addictive as MLP.

She opened the book, and her eyebrows popped up in surprise. "You really did this?"

"Yes!" I laughed. "Don't act so shocked."

"I'm miserable at drawing." She turned the pages, smiling at each sketch. "I can't imagine how amazing you'll be after you take classes."

"Thanks." Hearing Emma say I was amazing—I could get used to that. We seemed to have picked back up pretty easily after everything that had happened, and I was glad. It gave me enough confidence to ask her something I'd been afraid to on Friday. "So, I noticed last week that you don't actually get picked up by your mom after school."

Her eyes widened.

"I saw you walking home after you read your book. I just wondered why you'd lie to me about that. It's kinda weird."

Emma put her hands to her pink face and whimpered, "Can you just pretend you didn't find that out?"

"I really can't."

She hung her head, and her dark hair covered her face. "That first day of school, I was just going to check out the book and go home like I usually did, okay? My mom *does* work, so I read at home until she gets back. But then you caught me, and you knew about the book I was reading and it was nice to talk to you."

"So . . ." I was on the edge of my seat, dying to hear her say it.

"I wanted to keep talking to you, but I didn't want you to *know* I wanted to. So I lied and said I was waiting for my mom." She looked up, trying to be mad. "Are you happy now?"

"Yeah, I'm happy now." I was sure the grin on my face looked dumb, but Emma wanted to be around me from the beginning and that meant something to me. "I have to go now, though. My mom actually *is* waiting for me since my dad refuses to drive me to school."

"Oh." She frowned. "Does this mean you won't be here after school?"

"Maybe. We're still working out all the complications." My smile must have gotten goofier because she was sad I might not be here, and that was pretty awesome. "But Skye is here. She works on her clothes every day. You two could keep each other company."

"Did you plan this or something? For us to be friends again?"

"I admit I hoped for that." I stood, knowing Mom was probably worried about leaving Holly with Mrs. Jorgenson for too long. "See you later. We hang out in the art hall at lunch if you miss me and want to visit."

She rolled her eyes. "I don't *miss* you. But I will miss your phone."

"Ooh, burn." I laughed, said good-bye, and headed out to the front of the school feeling like a million bucks. Emma watched MLP, liked it, and was my friend again. Too much good outweighed the bad for me to even think about it.

I thought about what Skye had said before the meet-up, "No one can make you feel inferior without your consent."

I hadn't been doing that long, but my life had already changed.

Chapter 31

MOM DROVE TO Quincy's house to pick up Holly. It was the first time I'd been there since Quincy had laughed at me for liking MLP. I wasn't sure what to expect. From the texts I'd read on the way back from school, he was saying sorry but it didn't feel sincere.

I didn't want to be like Skye and Emma—not being friends with Quincy because of this one thing—but facing him seemed impossible. Or at least like something I preferred to avoid.

So when Mom pulled up to the Jorgensons' house, I seriously considered staying in the car and not dealing with it. But Mom would ask me what was up, and explaining it to her was slightly worse than facing it. I forced myself out of the car and up the stairs of the front porch. Mom rang the doorbell, and Mrs. Jorgenson appeared quickly.

"Hi!" she said cheerily. "Holly! Your mom and Drew are here to get you!"

"Noooooooo!" her shrill voice came from the living room. Behind that, I heard My Little Pony playing. "We're only halfway through the episode. Can we go after?"

Mrs. Jorgenson laughed as we walked toward Holly. "You were right—all I had to do was turn on that show and she was great."

"Oh good. I know she can be a handful."

"Aren't they all? She is adorable. Makes me wish I had a daughter."

When we entered the room, I was surprised Holly wasn't the only one sitting there. Quincy was, too. I figured he would have been upstairs playing video games and hiding from my "scary" little sister. But there he was, watching the show with her. I had no idea what to think.

"Drew!" Holly waved me over. "It's the one where Rainbow Dash picks a pet. Come watch with me."

I looked at Mom. "Hey, how 'bout I walk home with her after the episode?"

"That would be great!" Mom said, clearly tired from being out all day. She looked to Mrs. Jorgenson. "Of course, if that's okay with you."

"Not a problem at all." Mrs. Jorgenson headed for the kitchen, where she was prepping something for dinner. "Leave whenever you want. I don't mind all the company."

"Just stay for dinner," Quincy said out of nowhere. He hadn't looked at me yet—his eyes were still on the TV screen. On the ponies. "Might as well."

"Can you?" Mrs. Jorgenson asked. "I have more than enough."

Mom took a seat at the kitchen table, letting out a relieved sigh. "Oh, I'd love to not have to make dinner tonight. Scott won't be home until late anyway."

It looked like we'd be here much longer than I planned. While it felt uncomfortable, I gave in and sat on the couch by Holly. She nudged me. "Hey, get out your sketchbook. I need you to draw me Dash and Tank."

"Fine, fine." I grabbed my stuff, having no problem drawing for distraction. Quincy still hadn't said anything to me, and the longer it went the more awkward it felt. I didn't know what to make of him watching the show but not talking. He was perfectly still, no twitches, or tapping, or any other movements he always made.

So I got to drawing. I liked sketching Rainbow Dash, mostly her hair. She had cool hair that wasn't hard to draw like Rarity's or Pinkie Pie's. I liked that such a simple design still looked so good.

By the time I finished the basic outline of Dash and Tank, the episode finished. Holly pounced on the remote. "Another one?"

"Yes," I said at the same time as Quincy. I looked over at him, confused. "What?"

"Another one!" Quincy said. He looked at me briefly and then down at his hands. "It's not so bad. That pink one is funny. And the blue one is cool."

"Pinkie Pie and Rainbow Dash," Holly said, hitting play.

"I see. . . ." I smiled. Did Quincy seriously just say My Little Pony wasn't so bad? "So, did you just start watching today? Or before this?"

"Today," he said, eyes back on the screen where the next one was starting. "I figured, you know, since Holly was here and stuff, it wouldn't be so bad to watch it with her and see what all the fuss is about."

"And?" I said, enjoying this immensely.

"Well . . . it tricks you," he said, and then there was a long pause while he watched. "Like, it's all pink and stuff, but then there's that blue one holding a race for pets and being all tough. And the orange one is like this cowgirl. And they all fight evil and shit. That weird dragon-goat-thing in there was cool."

"Discord!" Holly said. "Just say their names! They aren't hard to remember."

I laughed. "Holly, he's not saying them because it makes him seem like he's still cool because he's not really paying attention."

"What?" Quincy looked at me. "I don't remember them!"

I looked at him flatly. "You have, like, a photographic memory."

Quincy pursed his lips, totally caught.

"Watch out," I said as I went back to my drawing. "If you keep this up, you'll be one of those pansy boys who likes My Little Pony. And you know how lame they are. It'd be the worst thing ever."

His shoulders slumped. "Okay, okay, I'm sorry, alright? I am an idiot sometimes."

"Sometimes?"

He put his finger to his lips. "Shh. Gosh, Drew, we're trying to watch a show here. It's not like you were nice that night either."

"Okay, yeah, sorry." I went back to my drawing, knowing this was Quincy's way of saying he had been a total jerk and that he should have given it a chance before being all judgy. I wasn't about to push it further—he was watching the show and not mocking it in the process.

Then it dawned on me that people had to *watch the show*. I'd seen it three times now—with Jake, Emma, and now Quincy. People thought My Little Pony was one thing, but when they saw how much deeper it went, they stopped being jerks about it.

So maybe if I got Dad to watch . . .

It was a nice thought, but not that simple. I could ask. I could dare him to until I was blue in the face, and he'd probably still refuse because it'd make him "less of a man."

But it *had* worked with other skeptics, which was something. I couldn't deny that it might be worth a shot, even if it was a ridiculously long shot that would probably blow up in my face.

Chapter 32

"OKAY," I SAID to Skye as she showed up to our lunch spot without food yet again. "You *need* to stop with the not eating lunch."

She made a face at me as she sat next to me. "None of us have time in the morning to make lunch. And I'm not going in that cafeteria. Ever."

"You are *starving*, Skye." She'd lost weight by only living off what I shared with her, and she was already thin enough. "And you don't even go home right away—you sew for like two hours. You can't keep running yourself into the ground like this. I know it's your passion and stuff, but you can't die for it."

She glared at me. "Are you my mom now?"

"If I have to be. Should I tell her what you're doing?"

"Don't you dare!" She looked from side to side, as if her mom could hear us. "I've been using the money she gives me to buy extra fabric."

"What?" My mouth gaped open. "She'll kill you!"

"I know! So shut up." Skye leaned back into the wall, grabbing her stomach. In the silence it growled.

I was tired of giving up part of my lunch. I was starving the rest of the day because of it. This had to stop. "You have to go buy lunch. Like right now."

"Drewwwwwww . . ." She held out the *w* sound until it turned into a horrible whine. "Don't make me do that. You know what it's like in there. You saw it. Teagan will find me. It's finally getting kind of quiet for us, and that's nice."

I sighed. She was right. It had been a couple weeks since everything had gone down on Homecoming night, and with our stealthy hideout and general avoidance of people who mocked us, we were surviving school pretty well lately. People had forgotten we were there, and that was about the best we could hope for.

But Skye was starving because of it. That wasn't exactly a good trade-off, starving to avoid being bullied, like putting a tiny bandage over a gaping wound.

"What if I go for you?" I asked.

"You'd do that for me?"

"Well . . . if we went together, they'd probably say something like we're a couple and find some way to make that gross. They'll probably give me crap alone, but I can deal." Plus, I didn't want Emma to hear people saying I was in a relationship with Skye. Skye was my friend, and I was pretty sure we both liked it that way.

"I feel bad making you do that for me," Skye said.

"Well, I feel bad watching you starve all day." I held out my hand. "Give me the money. I'm small and boring looking. I might not even be noticed."

She laughed a little, holding out the money. "Thanks, Drew. Sorry for this, but I'm really hungry and can't resist the offer."

"It's okay." I got up and tried to look courageous, although I knew I was about to walk into a minefield. But this was important for Skye's health. "I'll be back in a few minutes. Or if I'm not, I'm probably hiding from the jerks in a locker."

She raised an eyebrow. "You can fit in a locker?"

"Tall people, so entitled," I grumbled, walking off toward the cafeteria.

The closer I got to the hub of the school—the lunchroom and commons—the more people there were. I could tell they noticed me when I walked by, which didn't bode well. I forced myself not to pay attention to their expressions or their words. Food. I just had to get the food and get back. The rest didn't matter.

The line was almost finished when I got to the cafeteria, since lunch had started almost ten minutes before.

I slipped behind the last person and made myself as small and invisible as possible. Then I prayed Jake would know I needed him to distract the football players.

I grabbed a tray. Having no idea what Skye wanted, I picked food at random. She was probably so famished she'd eat anything, and she hadn't said anything about allergies I needed to worry about. I held out the money for the lunch server, got the change, and planned to get out of there in a hurry. Maybe people *had* forgotten about us. Maybe it would get better once people got over it.

A black shirt appeared in front of me.

I looked up. It was the guy who'd harassed Skye before—Teagan—and clearly he wasn't there to make friends.

"Hey, Pony Freak," he said, stepping so close his clothes were almost in Skye's food. "Where's your whack job sidekick?"

From experience I knew it was better not to reply, so I tried to move around him. One of his friends blocked me. I went to the other side, only to be stopped by his other lackey. I sighed. "Can you move, please?"

"Not until you give me Whack Job's phone number," he said.

As hard as I tried to stay neutral, my face contorted into disgust. He had to be kidding, and yet I didn't think he was. "Leave her the hell alone, psycho."

"Who knew?" He raised an eyebrow in amusement. "The sissy pony freak has some balls!"

His friends laughed.

Everyone in the entire cafeteria watched. I caught sight of Jake from the corner of my eye. He looked down at his food, clearly worried, and I knew I'd get no help from him. As much of a coward as I had been, he was way worse.

"Seriously, wuss." Teagan shoved my shoulder, almost making me drop Skye's food. "You think I don't know what's going on? You don't really like her—not like I do. You're just lying about liking that stupid show so you can get in her pants."

"What?" I said, much louder than I meant to.

"At least I'm honest," he went on. "I want a piece of her crazy ass and you're in the way. I ain't lying about it. Now give me her number, stop hanging out with her, and I'll be merciful."

Merciful. I'd heard that word many times before, usually as a precursor to getting beaten up, regardless of how hard I tried to placate the people threatening me. I didn't know why this time was different—why instead of inciting fear this guy just made me angry. I glared at him without remorse. "And what if I don't?"

"Well . . ." He swatted at the tray, knocking it to the ground. "Then no lunch for you, for starters."

I scoffed at him. "That was for Skye. She was too afraid of all you jerks to come get it herself. Good job, Romeo."

Teagan snapped. His eyes went into rage mode, and the fist came fast and hard right into my nose, not even going easy on the first hit. I stumbled back a bit, but remained standing at least. I felt the blood even before I put my hand to my face, warm and slick as it trickled down my chin.

He grinned, satisfied. I hated this guy. I hated even more that people thought it was okay for him to do this because I was small. The lunchroom staff headed our way—this guy would get in trouble for sure—but it wasn't enough. In that moment I was tired of grown-ups intervening, which only resulted in me getting hurt more. I was tired of being the one who people thought would roll over and take it. I was plain *exhausted* from taking the high road all the time.

I guess I snapped, too. It seemed like a good idea to shove my foot into his stomach.

So I did.

As hard as I could.

The guy hit the ground and stared at me, shocked. The whole school froze in time for a second, everyone's eyes on me and not even a whisper on anyone's lips.

"Being a Brony doesn't make me a sissy, asshole." Maybe it was dumb and immature, but I felt strong and proud of who I was. "And you better leave my friend alone."

I'd like to say that everyone in school cheered and no one ever messed with me or Skye again. But in reality, Teagan's friends pounced on me. They hit me in the face again and in the gut. They stomped on my feet and elbowed my ribs. It probably didn't last more than ten seconds before adults yelled for them to stop and they were pulled off me, but that was all it took. My head spun from the beating, and I was sure I was about to hit the ground until someone grabbed my arm.

"Are you okay?" a gentle, familiar voice said.

"Emma?" I could kind of see her, all blurry.

"Your nose." She put a napkin to it and squeezed.

"Thanks." I got my bearings back and noticed two teachers handling my attackers. Of course, one of them *had* to be my father, who looked at me like I was at fault.

Chapter 33

"TO THE OFFICE. Now." Dad's voice echoed through the cafeteria, followed by a ton of whispers. I wasn't sure how much he had seen, but part of me hoped he had witnessed me fighting back. He needed to learn I wasn't backing down either. "All of you."

"B-but it wasn't his fault!" Emma blurted out, holding me back. "They attacked him!"

"And he fought back," my father said with no emotion. "Zero tolerance policy."

"This is so un-Christian!" Emma yelled. "Then you should take the whole lunchroom to the office because they sat there and let it all happen! I guess I should go, too!"

"Do what you want, miss." My father dragged two of the guys towards the door. "Just make sure that one comes with you, or he'll be in worse trouble."

That one. He wouldn't even say my name. I started walking, and Emma held my arm like she was worried

I might fall over at any second. I pulled the napkin from my nose to see if it was still bleeding. My left eye felt swollen, but I knew it'd feel even worse in a couple hours.

"Are you okay?" Emma whispered.

"You should let go," I said.

"What?"

"If you help me any longer, people will start thinking you're a pony freak, too. And, well, obviously that might not be a good idea."

"So?" Emma tucked her dark hair behind her ear and looked at the crowd defiantly. "It's just wrong. All of it is wrong, and I'm sorry I let my own hang-ups get in the way of doing what was right. I can't stand by and watch anymore."

I smirked, which made my face ache. Emma was having her own moment, like when I had defended Skye in class even though it had ended my safety as a "football-related person." I wished I hadn't gotten beat up for it to happen. "So you're one of us now?"

"I might have always been," she said. "I just didn't know it."

We walked out of the lunchroom behind Dad and the guys who beat me up. Once in the hall, Skye came running up to us. Her eyes filled with horror as she took in my appearance. "What happened?"

"I wouldn't give Teagan your number," I said. "He wasn't happy about it."

Skye put her hands over her mouth. "I'm so sorry. I told you it was a bad idea. I'm fine going without lunch!"

"You're not eating?" Emma's voice was filled with concern. "Skye!"

Skye looked away, but kept pace with us to the office. "You know how it is, so don't start lecturing me."

Emma sighed. "She'd do this in elementary school, too. She skipped lunch and saved the money to buy toys."

"It was the only way I could get them!" Skye said. "We don't have money like you do."

"I know . . ." Emma said.

"And this *isn't* the same." Skye tipped her chin up. "I *would* buy lunch if I didn't get insulted every time. But I may as well use the money for something I like if I can't for food."

"I can't tell if you're fighting or not," I admitted as we entered the office. "But I'll take you talking at least. It's pretty entertaining."

"I'd poke you right now if you didn't look horrible," Skye said.

The office secretaries were in a frenzy contacting the administrators to deal with four boys who were in a totally one-sided fight. But before any of them showed up from their lunch breaks, the school nurse appeared, took one look at me, and said, "Oh my heavens! Let me get you cleaned up."

I was about to go, but Skye held me back. "One sec, I'm taking pictures."

"Okay . . ." I looked at her like she was crazy.

She glared at Teagan. "Just in case the principal doesn't think you look that hurt after the nurse wipes all that blood off."

"Is it a lot?" I asked as she snapped a couple pictures. It hadn't even occurred to me to think of what I looked like, but I was glad Skye had my back and made sure to get proof. She knew as well as I did how people played down bullying if they didn't have a record of it.

"It's pretty bad," Emma said, cringing.

"Huh. Had no clue." I'd gotten hit a lot in my life in football and then after. Maybe the pain had dulled over time. Or perhaps I knew that words hurt a lot more, and at least this time I hadn't let their words make me feel bad.

That was the biggest victory.

The nurse took me in and put a cold pack on my eye while she dabbed at the blood. She checked the other places where they had hit me to make sure I didn't have bruised ribs.

"Trust me, my ribs are fine," I told her. "I've broken them before, so I know how bad it hurts."

"I just need to be sure," she said. "I need to note all the injuries for the record."

I nodded. "I only hit Teagan once. I kicked him in the stomach."

"I see." That was all she said. I figured she had to keep a fairly unbiased stance even if it was clear I had been ganged up on.

After that, I came out to find Skye and Emma waiting for me. On the opposite side of the office, guarded by my dad and another teacher, stood Teagan and his friends. They glared at me, and I half expected them to flip me off when no one was looking.

"Everything okay?" Emma and Skye asked at the same time.

"Relatively speaking. Nothing's broken."

"That's good," Skye said. "We're staying so we can tell the principal what really happened."

"Yeah." It didn't escape my notice that Dad had hardly looked at me, probably ashamed that I had sullied his good name even more. "And you might wanna get a restraining order on Teagan because he's stalking you basically."

"I've thought about it," she admitted.

Emma frowned. "Maybe I should walk home with you, Skye."

"That would be nice." The moment Skye said it, they both looked like two peas in a pod. "I'd feel a lot safer."

"You know what?" I said, smiling even if it hurt my face. "Friendship totally *is* magic."

They looked at me for a split second before laughing their heads off. Then I laughed, too, and even though I was in this horrible situation, it didn't feel so bad. I had them. The rest of the school didn't matter. Whatever happened next didn't matter.

"Where in the world did that come from?" Emma asked.

I shrugged.

The principal appeared from her office. She did not seem happy to have her lunch interrupted by this drama. "Andrew Morris?"

"Here." I stepped forward.

"You're first." She looked at the other guys. "I'll speak with you each individually in order to see how the stories line up. Mr. Morris, make sure they don't talk amongst themselves while I'm speaking with Andrew."

"Yes, ma'am," my father said. Then he nodded at me. "Don't go easy on that one, either. He coulda avoided all this if he wanted."

All the good feelings disappeared with his cutting words. He blamed this on me. In his head I had started the fight by being there and making myself a target with my sissy interests. If I weren't so pathetic, I wouldn't be a victim.

I felt like kicking him in the stomach, too.

"This way, Andrew." The principal went into her office, and I took the first available chair as she closed the door. She sat in front of me and watched me for a few seconds. I had to hand it to her, she did seem neutral at least. "I was told there was a fight in the lunchroom."

I nodded. "Yes, ma'am. Sorry, ma'am."

"Do you know our policy on violence at school?"

I shook my head.

"Even if it's a first offense, you will receive punishment—detention and possibly suspension if I determine it suitable. There are no exceptions. Do you understand?"

"Yes, ma'am." This wasn't surprising, but it did suck. I was the one who had gotten beat unfairly, and yet because I had defended myself, I'd be punished, too. Would I have to be in detention with all of them? That would sure be fun.

"Tell me what happened in your own words."

I explained the situation, why I went to the cafeteria and how Teagan threatened both me and

Skye. I told her I wasn't going to risk Skye's safety to get out of there, and I admitted to kicking Teagan after he bloodied my nose. The principal took notes throughout my story, not asking a single question.

"Thank you," she said when I finished. "A couple questions."

"Okay . . ."

"How long have you and Skye been bullied about this?"

I sunk in my chair, not expecting it to go this direction. "Uh, she's been harassed about it from the first day of school. Me? Since I stood up for her a month ago and admitted I liked the show."

"Has Teagan been one of her harassers for a long time?"

"I think so. I don't know all the details . . ." I touched my phone in my pocket, remembering the video I had of his threats about Homecoming. Never had I gone so far to stand up for myself, but this wasn't me—it was Skye. And after what I'd seen from Teagan, I had to. "But, well, I took this video. This was before we were friends and when I really started worrying about her."

I pulled it up and showed it to the principal. As she watched Skye being pinned to the lockers, she was now clearly concerned. "Thank you for showing me this, Andrew. How do you feel about emailing this video to me? I might need it as I investigate what's going on here."

"Sure." I sent it to her school email address as she directed.

"I think that's it for now," she said, standing. "Once I've heard from the other boys I will let you know how long your detention will be."

"Okay." I walked out with her, feeling slightly relieved that she had said detention and not suspension.

I waited until everyone had given their stories, which ended up going well into the class after lunch. My father left to teach and was replaced with another beefy teacher who coached the wrestling team. Once everyone talked, we waited for our sentences. I then went back into the principal's office

She handed me a peach-colored sheet of paper with DETENTION SCHEDULE printed on top. Two more peach sheets were on her desk, plus a red one. Although I didn't know what red meant, it seemed bad. "Considering all the circumstances, I've decided that you will have two weeks of detention. I wish you would have come to the administration sooner with what has been going on. Next time, please talk to me instead of kicking people, okay?"

"Yes, ma'am." I looked over the sheet. An hour and a half detention after school every day didn't seem so bad, considering I'd been here after school since day one anyway.

"You may go."

I left as fast as I could. I would have kept going all the way to Emma and Skye and out of the office, but Miss Overly appeared. She was not smiling like usual. "Drew, may I talk to you?"

"Uh, sure." I stepped inside her office, not knowing what to expect after what had happened. But I hoped it wasn't what I thought it was. "Do I have to get counseling because of this or something?"

"No. Though it never hurts." She looked at her door like she was wrong to talk to me. "But, well, your father spoke with me."

"He did?" For a second my heart soared, like maybe this was proof he cared about me on some level. Maybe he couldn't express it himself, and he still watched out for me in some way. "What'd he say?"

"He said you'd changed your mind about pursuing art, that you wanted your schedule changed back to how it was," she explained with marked skepticism in her voice. "It seemed odd to me, since you were so excited about it the other day. I thought I would check before I reverted anything."

I let out a dry, short laugh. What was I thinking? Here I'd been beat up, so of course, he tried to ruin my life more. "No, I don't want those changes. He lied to you because he thinks I'm a pansy for liking art."

"I see." Miss Overly put a hand on my shoulder. "Don't take this the wrong way, but maybe now I am recommending you come see me. All of this can't be easy."

"It's not," I admitted. "I'll think about it."

Because at this rate, Dad would drive me crazy, crazier than all the jerks in the school combined. But it wasn't me who needed therapy. I was pretty sure he did—and I planned on telling him that.

Chapter 34

I STOOD OUTSIDE on our front lawn, holding a football and waiting for Dad to come home. My detention would start tomorrow—which would jack up my schedule yet again—so this was my only chance to confront him.

I had it all planned out. First, I would tell him he was wrong to blame me for what had happened today. I was the victim. Not that he would believe me, but I decided I had to stick up for myself at least. My face was swollen and bruised, may as well. He couldn't hit me when I looked like this.

Then I'd tell him that I knew he had tried to change my schedule, and explain how messed up he was to take my dream from me. The more I thought about it, the angrier I got. He had no right to stop me from taking art—he was completely out of line. Maybe if I explained how much I liked it, how it made me happy, he'd get over it.

And then, after all that, I'd dare him to watch My Little Pony. He'd get mad for sure, but it was only fair that he knew what he insulted. It was one thing not to like it after seeing it, but another entirely to judge it without even trying to understand.

Of course, first I had to get him to look at me long enough to say any of this. That's what the football was for. I figured maybe we could play catch. He liked stuff like that.

I didn't mind it so much either. As I tossed the ball from one hand to the other, I remembered a time when Dad had talked to me and we'd thrown this thing back and forth. I had liked those parts of my ill-fated football life the most, just throwing the ball for fun with no pressure or expectation. I wouldn't mind doing that again, if he'd let me.

The sun had set, and the light was going quickly when his truck appeared on the horizon. I prepped myself. This was no big deal. I wanted to talk to my dad, to stand up for myself and ask him to understand me. That's what I was supposed to do as a son, wasn't it?

He pulled into the gravel driveway, and the headlights blocked my vision of him. Surely he saw me—I was right there with a spotlight on me.

The truck's engine turned off, and Dad stepped out. He didn't look at me for even a millisecond. I thought the football would *at least* get me half a second. He walked toward the house like I was a ghost he didn't know was there.

"Hey, Dad!" I started. "I thought maybe we could—"

Slam.

He was in the house before I finished the first sentence. I stood there, stunned, but then anger flared in my chest. I went after him, right to the kitchen since he would probably go for dinner. But he wasn't there. Mom was putting leftovers on a plate.

"Where's Dad?" I asked.

"Said he was tired," she replied as she put the food in the microwave. "Went upstairs to rest."

"So that's how it's gonna be." I took a deep breath. "I'll take that food up to him."

She raised an eyebrow. "What happened?"

"Nothing."

She folded her arms, ignoring the microwave beep. "Since when do you ever voluntarily go see your father?"

I cringed, knowing I didn't have a good answer. Mom knew about the fight today, both from my wounds and from the school calling. I spent most of the drive home telling her about it, how Teagan had harassed Skye, and how I felt like I had to stand up for her and me. She wasn't happy, but it seemed like she understood.

But I hadn't told her what Dad had done. It meant a lot to me . . . and yet, it was also not that big of a deal. He hadn't gotten my classes changed. Everything was still on course for next semester. But the *idea* that he'd gone to that length, that hurt so much.

"Andrew Scott Morris," Mom said sternly. "What are you hiding?"

I sighed. No avoiding it now—she knew something was up and she'd hound me until I told her. "When I was in the office today, after all the fight stuff got sorted out, Miss Overly talked to me. She told me Dad wanted her to change my schedule back to what it was, but she wanted to check with me first."

Mom looked absolutely disgusted. "Is that the truth?"

"That's what Miss Overly said." I put my hands in my pockets, withdrawing. She looked so angry I worried she'd lash out at me. "It's just art, I don't get why it bothers Dad so much."

"Because he's being an idiot." Mom went to the microwave, grabbed the food, and pointed at me. "You stay here. *I'm* talking with him about this."

She stomped out of the kitchen, mumbling something under her breath I didn't catch. Her feet pounded up the stairs, the bedroom door opened and slammed shut, and I heard muffled-but-obvious yelling from both my parents. It reminded me of the time when I was in the hospital and my mother had put down the ultimatum that I wasn't playing football anymore.

Except it seemed worse this time. I wasn't in a hospital. I was a bit banged up, and Dad's attempts to stop me from pursuing art frustrated me, but this was not a life-threatening situation. And they still yelled at each other.

They yelled at each other a lot.

When they weren't yelling, they snapped at each other.

Or no interaction at all.

I leaned on the kitchen counter as reality sunk in. I'd been so focused on my own problems—on figuring out what I wanted in life, on accepting that I liked MLP, on making friends with Emma and Skye—that I hadn't thought about how many problems my parents had.

CRASH.

The sound of breaking glass jarred me out of my thoughts. In the silence of the house, my father's voice boomed, "GET THE HELL OUT!"

"You first!" Mom's voice was much quieter, but still clear.

Chills ran down my spine, and guilt filled my stomach. I shouldn't have told her what had happened. This fight wouldn't have existed if I'd kept it to myself. What if they were serious? What if they split up? While I hated my dad . . . I didn't want that.

"Drew?" Holly popped her head into the kitchen, and I saw her tears. "I'm scared. Can you stay with me?"

"Yeah." I had forgotten that if I could hear all the yelling, so could my little sister. If I was worried, Holly was probably terrified. I went to the living room with her, and she grabbed onto me tightly. She hadn't been this close to me ever, but I held her and tried to be strong.

She watched My Little Pony, the show that had started the fight. I didn't know how to feel about watching it while my parents yelled about this very thing upstairs. All I'd wanted to do was figure out my life and be happy—I had no idea it would make my parents so *un*happy with each other.

"What if they keep fighting?" Holly said quietly.

I gulped, knowing I couldn't say the D word to an eight-year-old. She'd lose it. I was kind of losing it even. "They'll work it out."

"How do you know?" she asked. "They might not."

"They have before. It'll be okay." I squeezed her arm. "Don't worry."

Holly nodded into my stomach, and I felt my shirt getting wet from her tears. "Will you at least be my big brother best friend forever? You won't go, right?"

My laugh was pained. Holly definitely knew her MLP references. "Sure, as long as you stay my little sister best friend forever."

"I promise," she said.

I squeezed my eyes shut on the tears forming there. Maybe my parents were fighting upstairs, but I had Holly. I couldn't have said that at the beginning of the school year. I hadn't felt close to any of my family, but now Holly and I were real family. And the same show was ruining the other half of my family.

Honestly, I didn't know what to do or how to fix it and still keep the things I'd come to love. And if I didn't figure it out soon, I'd lose it all either way.

Chapter 35

DETENTION WAS WORSE than I thought it'd be. Mostly because I couldn't use my phone, so therefore I didn't have Skye or Quincy to entertain me through texting. Emma asked if she could hang out in the detention room with me, but that wasn't allowed either. So it was me and two of the guys who'd hit me a few days ago.

Teagan had been suspended.

Apparently Skye spent extra time with the principal recounting the creepiness she'd suffered from Teagan. The school wanted to get him serious counseling outside of school. As Skye said, he was "legit messed up." It made me feel kind of bad for him, but not bad enough to think he didn't deserve it all.

"Okay, guys, you're free," said Mr. Rivera. He was on detention duty this time. It had been a different teacher each day of the week. "Go and sin no more."

One of Teagan's lackeys groaned. "You're not funny."

"Now you know how people feel when you joke around," Mr. Rivera replied.

I smirked, but said nothing. I wanted to get out as much as they did, so I rushed for the door. Just one more week. I could survive that.

Emma waited outside for me, and she smiled when our eyes met. "Hey."

"Hey." I looked around but saw no girl wearing brightly colored pony clothing. "Did Skye leave?"

Emma shook her head. "Still in the Home Ec room. She said she had to finish something today and figured I could handle picking you up from detention all on my own."

"The next Brony meet-up is coming up. She probably wants to show it there." We walked toward the art hall. Since I had detention, it only complicated my schedule even more. Mom couldn't wait for me that long, so I ended up hanging out at Skye's until Dad got home and she could come get me.

It hadn't escaped me that this schedule was rough on Mom and definitely not sustainable. If I went to the high school I was supposed to, she wouldn't have to drive two hours every day to get me. Problem was, I liked being at Yearling High now. I didn't want to leave my friends and go back to the people who had bullied me for years. If being bad at football was enough to get me beat up, adding MLP on top of it would make it even worse.

Of course . . . if my parents kept fighting, I might not have a choice at all.

"Hey," Emma snapped me out of my thoughts. We were almost to the Home Ec room, and I hadn't even noticed. "Are you okay?"

I sighed. "Not really."

"What's up?"

"My parents are still fighting a lot. Mostly about me," I admitted. Talking to Emma made it a bit easier, at least until I thought about how I would lose her and Skye. "I'm a home wrecker. Because I like My Little Pony."

She frowned. "C'mon, it's not your fault."

"Sure feels like it though." I'd seen enough TV shows to know this was what people told kids of divorced parents, and here I was already getting it. Talk about foreshadowing.

"Also, it sounds completely stupid that so much drama could come from watching one show," Emma said. "Now I know why you thought I was overreacting."

I smiled, remembering how we'd watched episodes during lunch on my phone. Emma had brought Skye lunch from home and hung out with us more. It was pretty awesome. "Though, well, it turns out you were kind of right to avoid it all and just keep lying to your parents."

"I guess so," she conceded. "Though I do wish I could go to that meet-up with you and Skye. It sounds fun."

"Yeah, it is." I pulled at my shirt collar, feeling uncomfortable since I hadn't exactly told Skye that I couldn't go with her this time. She figured I would—we had signed up to make that rainbow cake—but with my parents at war I was scared to ask Mom if I could go. She would probably say yes, but if Dad heard that . . .

When we entered the Home Ec room, Skye was at the fabric-cutting table holding up a shirt covered in pink, yellow, and blue fringe. It might have been too much, but the way she arranged the colors diagonally made it look cool. Pinkie Pie would have certainly approved. She smiled as she shook it a little to show the movement. "What do you think, guys?"

"It's a party in a shirt," I replied.

Emma laughed. "That's the perfect description."

"That's *exactly* what I was going for." She set it down on the table, eyeing it with pride. "I've been doing a lot of casual wear—thought I could try my hand at some more special occasion pieces."

"Cool." Emma leaned on the table and touched the fringe. "What are you pairing it with?"

"I was thinking a white pencil skirt and hot pink heels," Skye said. "So it's fun but still a bit mature?"

Emma nodded. "That's awesome. I'd wear it even if I didn't know about the show."

Skye beamed, and they went on about fashion stuff I had no clue about. The terms only vaguely sounded familiar thanks to Rarity. It sure hadn't taken these two long to get back into their old friendship. They were clearly a good pair who never should have been apart. It was fun watching them, and it made me feel like I had at least done one thing right.

After Skye packed up, we started to walk to her house. Emma lived five houses down, but we never went the rest of the distance with her. Emma didn't want her parents to see us accidentally.

There was a time when I'd have fought her on that, but currently, I thought she was much smarter than me. Besides, if she ever decided to be honest with her parents, it should be her choice on the timing. It sucked to be outed before you were ready.

"Hey, so we need to get the ingredients for the rainbow cake," Skye said to me. "I have a little money, but if you could split the cost in half with me that'd be great."

I gulped. Here was the opening, and I had to take it. "Yeah, I can definitely pay for half and help make it, but I actually don't think I'll be able to go that night."

"What?" Skye stopped walking. "But your parents know! Are they seriously not gonna let you go? Your mom seems so nice!"

"It's just . . ." I put my hands in my pockets, hating to say it because I wanted to go and none of this was fair. But I couldn't think about myself and what I wanted anymore. "Every time I bring up something pony-related, my parents fight. So I haven't even asked my mom, and I kind of don't want to. My little sister freaks out when they get mad. It's all so ugly and I'm tired of it."

Skye's shoulders slumped. "That's not fair. I can't even fight with that."

"Sorry," I said. "But I can still help with the cake. I mean, since I'll be here waiting for my mom anyway."

"Fine, I guess I'll just have to deal. Everyone will be so sad you're not there." We started walking again and were almost to her house. "And don't say they won't notice—Tyler and Frankie notice *everyone*."

I smirked. "How'd you know I would say that?"

"Because you think people don't see you," Emma said. She looked away from me, embarrassed. "But they do."

"It's true," Skye continued. "You stand out. That's why you get bullied. My mom keeps promising me that after high school being different will be an asset, but I'm not sure I believe it."

"I didn't until I met Tyler and Frankie," I admitted. "They seem really happy and no one at that college cared about the meet-up."

"Good point." Skye stepped onto the grass. "See you later, Emma. Hope you can come someday, too."

Emma nodded, smiling sadly. "Maybe when I'm old enough to drive."

"So, a year! I'm holding you to it." Skye pulled out her keys, and we waved good-bye to Emma. Then we were inside making something for dinner. After a week of this, it had begun to feel normal, kind of like going to Quincy's but with more work. I never had to take the trash out at Quincy's, and yet here I helped out—especially when I was eating their food and they were scraping by. It was the least I could do.

Harley and Ms. Zook got home at about the same time every night, and we ate while Harley told us everything he did at work. He had the best stories, about crying little kids he gave suckers to, about how gross it was to clean up broken eggs, about how to bag groceries properly. I don't know how he did it, but he made the most boring things sound exciting.

"And then the grandma was trying to pick up this giant—*giant*—box of . . ." The doorbell rang, and he frowned at the interruption. "Oh man! Your mom's here, Drew."

"Yeah, sorry. I better go." I stood up from the kitchen table and grabbed my backpack.

"She can come in, you know," Ms. Zook said. "We'd be happy to have more company."

"Thanks." I bit my lip, looking toward the front door. "It's just that it's kind of a long drive, and my little sister doesn't like it when my mom has to leave her."

"I understand," she replied. "Maybe we can all get together sometime at your place on the weekend."

I tried not to look horrified by the proposal. Dad would *love* for me to bring even more "pony freaks" home. I'm sure he'd act like I'd brought zombies into the house. "We'll have to see. Bye."

"See you on Monday!" Skye said.

"Yup."

Heading to the door, I opened it and Mom was there smiling widely. But that wasn't all—she also had puffy, red eyes, which meant she had been crying. "Hey, sugar! Wanna grab a milkshake on the way home? I need a milkshake."

"Sure, sounds good."

I determined to ignore what Mom was hiding. She didn't seem to want to talk about it anyway. But as we grabbed our milkshakes and drove home chatting about superficial things, the pit of guilt in my stomach only grew. By the time we hit our driveway, I couldn't go inside without losing it and starting another fight.

"Hey, is it okay if I stay over at Quincy's tonight?" I asked. It was short notice, but his parents were usually cool with it.

"That sounds like a good idea," she said. "Tell Mrs. Jorgenson thanks for being so hospitable, okay?"

"Of course." The car stopped, and I got out. Instead of going inside to grab stuff, I headed immediately to the field and Quincy's house in the distance. I'd survive a night of not brushing my teeth if it meant I didn't have to see Dad or hear him insult me and Mom.

Pulling out my phone, I texted Quincy a warning. *Coming over now. Did you save me pizza?*

His reply was swift. *There's some left. Hurry or I'll eat it.*

Almost there. I smiled. At least Quincy was on board—he'd watched almost the whole MLP series now, but he wasn't sold on the Equestria Girls. Said he had to draw the line somewhere.

I only had to knock twice before he opened the door and let me in. Letting out a deep breath, I said, "It still smells like pizza in here."

"It's on the kitchen table."

Although I'd had dinner at Skye's and a milkshake with my mom, I grabbed a piece of pepperoni pizza and ripped into it. Guilty or not, I hadn't lost my appetite. In fact, it might have grown in the past month.

"So," Quincy said with a sly smile. "How's your herd of girls?"

I rolled my eyes. He'd admitted to being jealous that my friends at Yearling High were two cute girls, so I let the dig slide. "They're good. I'm the one with all the problems these days. Too bad you don't go to school there, too. Then we'd really be a herd."

"I've been thinking about it, actually."

I paused mid-bite, pizza hanging out of my mouth. I couldn't have heard that right. Quincy wanted to go to school with me? "Are you serious?"

He shrugged. "Half the homeschoolers are in high school now and making other friends. It's been really boring around here with you gone all day all the time. And, I don't know, I'm fifteen but I'm almost a junior class-wise. If I didn't like it, it'd only be, like, a few semesters."

I swallowed my bite. "You can't just say something like that and not do it. I never hoped you'd go to school with me, and if you take it away now, I would hate you."

He laughed. "Well, it'd be next semester."

"Too bad you weren't doing it sooner," I said. "Then I could convince your mom to take us to the Brony meet-up instead of putting my mom in a bad spot again. And we could switch driving to school. It'd make it so much easier to—"

"Wait." Quincy held up his finger. "Back it up. There's another Brony meet-up? When?"

"Next Friday," I said. "They're every month."

"You going with the girls?"

"It's just Skye . . . but I'm not going." I looked at the pizza crust in my hand, suddenly not that hungry. While I'd told Emma and Skye about my parents fighting, I hadn't gone into much detail with Quincy. We were neighbors—I didn't think Mom would want the neighborhood finding out. "You know my dad. He's still pissed about everything and won't let me."

"I wanna go!" Quincy said.

"What? You were laughing at me last time!"

"Well, last time I didn't know the show was cool and that I could make friends with cute girls." Quincy went over to the couch in the living room and sat down. I followed. "What if I met you after school and we went? My mom would drive us—my parents don't care at all that I like it."

"Lucky."

He flipped through the guide on the TV, looking for whatever interested him tonight. "I guess when your kid has Tourette's, you get over judging people too much."

"I guess so." Now that Quincy had planted the seeds of hope in my mind, I couldn't help pursuing the possibilities. "You think your mom could really take us? Because if she can, I might actually be able to go. Skye was so bummed when I told her I couldn't. We were supposed to make this cake and stuff."

He raised an eyebrow. "A cake, huh?"

"We signed up for food duty."

"Interesting. I like food." He stopped on some anime show. "So do you want me to ask my mom, like, right now or something?"

"Yes." Because this could be the best of both worlds. I wouldn't be a noob like last time, and I'd tell Mom where I was, and we could pretend I was hanging out with Quincy like always. No fighting necessary.

Quincy pulled out his phone to text his mom upstairs. A moment later she replied. He smiled. "See? No problem. She'll do it."

"Awesome." Now I had to find the right time to tell Mom.

Chapter 36

ON SUNDAY AFTERNOON, Dad was on the sofa watching football with the volume on high while my mother worked in the kitchen making homemade rolls for dinner. Holly was up in her room pouting about not being able to watch her show. She, shockingly enough, never got grief for disliking football. This was the perfect time. Dad would be so engrossed he'd never hear. Holly was gone and wouldn't blurt out my plans.

I'd thought about texting Mom to ask if I could go to the Brony meet-up with Quincy, but I worried Dad would somehow see the text. They popped up on the phone screen for all to see. Or maybe he checked her phone sometimes like he checked mine. Either way, I figured talking in person would be the best way to leave no tracks.

So I casually walked by Dad, and when I stepped into the kitchen I said as loudly as I could, "Hey, Mom! When's dinner gonna be done? I'm starving."

Mom glared at me. "When the rolls are done rising, so not for awhile."

"Aww, man!" I came closer to her, and she jumped in surprise. I lowered my voice. "Actually, I have something to ask you."

She looked to both sides, catching on to what I was doing. "What is it?"

"There's this . . . *thing* I want to go to."

"Thing?"

"Yeah." I looked over my shoulder. My "safe" plan wasn't feeling so foolproof right now. "You know, that thing I went to the night I, uh, went missing?"

"Oh! Oh . . ." Mom cringed. "Sugar, I don't know—"

"Quincy wants to come, too," I said quickly. "Mrs. Jorgenson said she'd drive, so you don't have to worry about a thing. I wasn't even going to ask, but when he said he could . . . would it be so bad? I'll just be out with Quincy, and you can relax, pretend we're at a movie."

She smiled sadly. "I'm afraid there's still a lot for me to worry about."

"I know." I hung my head, wondering if I should have asked at all. "I'm sorry. It's all my fault."

"What?" Mom stopped kneading the dough, her eyes wide. "Did you just say this was *your* fault?"

"Well, yeah . . ." I shouldn't have said that either. Suddenly, this felt like a bad idea. I wanted to go to the meet-up too badly, and I should have accepted that I couldn't. "You and Dad fight about me all the time. Holly and I aren't deaf."

"Whoa, back up one second." She picked up the dough and put it in the bowl. This meant I was going to get a talking-to. "This is *not* your fault. You found something you like to do because of a show you like to watch—that is a fantastic thing! It is not your problem that your father has the most narrow view possible on 'being a man.' I've spent *years* trying to get that through his thick skull, and I'll keep trying till I'm blue in the face."

Mom said I wasn't in trouble, but it didn't feel that way. "But if I *wasn't* interested in this stuff, then you guys wouldn't be fighting about it. So you can say it's not my fault, but it kinda is."

"It's not!" She let out a frustrated grunt. "You know what? Screw this. You're going to that Brony meet-up." Clearly looking for a fight, my mother raised her voice. "You are going to that Brony meet-up and no one can stop you!"

"Mom!" While I knew she was being supportive, in that moment I felt betrayed. I didn't want Dad to hear, and she made sure he did.

The sound cut off on the TV.

Dad's footsteps pounded towards us.

They would probably divorce after this, and the world would end, and I'd lose the things I liked most about my life. This was not how it was supposed to go. Why couldn't she have said yes or no quietly and let it go unnoticed?

"Did I hear something about them stupid-ass ponies?" Dad said, his voice raised.

"I'm taking Drew to the Brony meet-up on Friday," Mom's voice was polite and sugary sweet. "Holly would love it, so you'll just have to fend for yourself when you get home."

Dad clenched his jaw. "Did you forget the boy is grounded?"

"I'm *un*grounding him." She put her hands on her hips. I was about to witness the fights they usually kept in their room. "He would have asked to go last time if he knew you supported him. So it's *your* fault he went missing, not his."

Dad pointed to me. "He got in a *fight* last week! Was that my fault, too? He's still grounded."

"He was defending himself! Just like he has to defend himself with you," Mom shot back. "You're always sayin' he should be tougher, and then he stands up to these bullies and you switch stories."

"Fighting, disappearing, lying—and you think this crap he likes is good for him? So if he liked drugs, we should support that, too?"

"My Little Pony is NOT drugs! Drawing is NOT drugs! That's the dumbest comparison I ever heard!" Mom's voice was loud now, and I was sure Holly heard it. If she came down here . . .

"Mom, Dad, please stop figh—"

"It's *worse* than drugs!" Dad said, not even seeing me now. "If he was on drugs, at least people wouldn't think he was a freak of nature."

Mom scoffed. "If you haven't noticed yet, you're the only one who thinks that! He has *friends*, Scott. More than just Quincy. And they're cute girls! He has dreams and people are inviting him to things and he's happy—this is exactly what we wanted for him when we decided to move schools!"

"He's getting bullied just like before. You want that?" Dad glowered at her. "This is all your fault, brainwashing him and letting him watch girly stuff. Stop trying to make him into a sissy."

I partially stopped listening. What Dad said hit me like a ton of bricks. Just like with the football thing, he blamed this on Mom. He didn't see her as supporting me, but as the enemy who conned me into liking something I shouldn't. If I didn't speak up now, he'd spend the rest of his life blaming this on her like he did before.

"That's enough!" I yelled over them.

They stopped and looked at me as if they just realized I was still in the kitchen.

"Stop talking like I'm not right here. I'm sick of this! Talk to *me*! This is about *me*. You're both blaming it on each other and pretending like it'll get fixed if you leave me out of it and it won't." I pointed to my father, glaring at him. "This is *not* Mom brainwashing me. I love to draw—that was my decision and she didn't even know about it for awhile. Only Holly did. Stop trying to blame her for what you hate about me. Take it out on me."

Mom teared up. "Drew, you don't have to—"

"Mom, I'm glad you support me," I said gently. "But please stop picking fights with Dad to show that support. You can't make him change. I can't make him change. I wish he would be okay with everything, but I'm starting to learn that it's okay if people aren't okay with me. Like you said, I have friends. I have you and Holly. I don't need the whole world or even my own father to accept me. . . ."

"You don't need me to accept you, huh?" Dad cut in. "Fine. You want me to take it out on you?"

I almost said, "Bring it." But instead I waited for him to continue.

"You're not going to that damn freak show meeting. Why? Because you've underminded me in every possible way." Dad came closer, but it didn't bother me. At least he was taking it out on the right person now instead of Mom. "And you may not need my acceptance, but you *do* need my permission. Because you're a kid, and I'm your father."

"My permission doesn't count?" Mom said.

"Shut up!" He didn't even look at her. "You want me to blame you? Okay, it's your fault, Son. You could have picked another sport. You could have worked harder to become stronger. You could have been a *man,* but instead you quit football, got bullied for being a loser, and then you start watching a little girl show and drawing ponies like a sissy. You deserved to get hit for that shit. They beat me to it."

On the night he laid into me after the first Brony meet-up, his words had cut. This was equally cruel, but for some reason, it didn't have the same impact. Instead, I felt sad.

I pitied him.

"Scott, how can you say that?" Mom said as she covered her mouth, broken to pieces at this point. I guessed his words cut her this time instead of me.

"Mom, it's okay," I said, standing as tall as I could to face my father. I wouldn't do this out of anger or out of fear. This time I wouldn't let him make me feel inferior. "May I ask you a question, Dad?"

"Go ahead," he spat.

"Do you think Walt Disney is a sissy?"

His brow furrowed. "What?"

"I'm just sayin' . . . he's a famous animator and he was a man. He created movies about princesses and talking mice. He also became super rich because of it and is famous to this day even though he's dead." I had read about animators recently, not just the ones behind My Little Pony, but people like Walt Disney and Hayao Miyazaki and John Lasseter. All guys. All artists. "So, was Disney a sissy?"

"Yes," he answered, but it didn't sound too confident.

"What about John Lasseter, the creator of Pixar?" I continued. "He didn't make princess movies. He's done cars and toys and fish and stuff. Is he a sissy, too?"

"Just what in the hell are you trying to say?"

"I just want to know!" I held up my hands. "Because by your definition of being a man, I'm thinking at least 90 percent of the guys out there you'd call sissies. Artists, actors, musicians, dancers, writers . . . basically any guy who doesn't play sports or like them much, right?"

Silence. This was not the usual reply for my father.

"Or is it just that I was drawn to My Little Pony that bothers you?" I continued. "If I had watched some boyish cartoon and decided to be an artist, would it have been different? Is it the act of drawing that is so bad or the subject matter?"

"Both," he said. "But especially that stupid show."

"How do you know it's stupid? You've never watched it." At that moment, I caught movement out of the corner of my eye. I turned, seeing honey curls and part of Holly's face peeking out from behind the wall. Tearstains streaked her face. "Holly, go upstairs. I'll be up soon."

She shook her head, looking at Dad. "Why is My Little Pony stupid, Daddy?"

Dad's eyebrows popped up, and we looked to him for an answer. "Well, uh, sweetie, it's okay for you because you're a little girl."

Holly stepped further into the kitchen, her confusion only deepened by his answer. I knew the feeling. "So it's okay for little girls to watch stupid shows, but boys aren't allowed? Why?"

"Well—er—" Dad scratched the back of his neck, clearly struggling to find an answer when faced with his eight-year-old daughter. "Boys and girls are just different."

"Watch it, Scott," Mom said through her teeth. "If you tell my little girl she's lesser in any way, I will lose it."

I had to hand it to Holly, she had backed Dad into a corner better than I had. This was my chance to take it even further. "You let Mom and Holly watch those superhero movies with us. Aren't those 'boy shows'?"

"Yeah," Holly said with a nod. "Why did you do that?"

"It's okay if you watch boy shows," Dad said. "But Drew shouldn't watch girl shows."

Holly scrunched her face like she smelled bad cheese. "That's just stupid."

"Isn't it?" I said, putting my hands on her shoulders. "I think we should both be allowed to watch 'girl' and 'boy' shows."

She nodded. "It's not fair to the boys. They miss half of the good shows."

I couldn't help smiling at that.

"This ain't gonna work," Dad said. He was still angry and clearly trying to tiptoe around Holly.

"But Daddy," Holly said. "My Little Pony isn't even a stupid show. Even Chip Pullman at school saw it and said it was cool, and he plays football and everything. Just like you."

"Gary Pullman's boy?" Dad said in surprise. "Does his father know?"

Holly shrugged.

An idea formed in my head. It was a long shot, but there was no better time to go for it. "How about we make a deal, Dad?"

"A deal?" Dad looked down on me like he preferred to yell instead. "What kind of deal?"

"You watch the first two episodes of My Little Pony and—"

"Nope!" He waved his hands in front of himself. "No way in hell I'll do that."

"I'm not finished," I said. "If you watch, and you hate it, I won't go to the Brony meet-ups. None of them."

He froze, his interest piqued. "Go on."

"But if you like it—even just the tiniest bit—you let me go and drop all this once and for all." I gulped. This was a big gamble. Chances were, if we got him to watch, he'd hate every second. "You can't keep judging the show without even seeing any of it. So that's the deal. Take it or leave it. If you don't, you can keep fighting until you get a divorce."

Holly squeaked. "A divorce? You're getting divorced?"

"No, sugar . . ." Mom glanced at Dad, and I could tell she'd thought about it. A lot.

Holly must have sensed the lie, too, because she started bawling. "But if you get a divorce, we won't live together anymore! We won't be a family anymore!"

"Shh." Dad hated crying. He especially hated Holly crying. So this was perfect because he said, "Don't cry, baby girl. I'll watch the show, okay?"

"Really?" Holly perked right up, wiping her tears as quickly as turning off a faucet. I had to hand it to her—she might be the one to save us all in the end. She at least had given us a fighting chance.

Chapter 37

AS WE SAT down in the living room and Holly happily grabbed the remote, I had to admit that I never thought this would happen. All of us—*Dad* included—sitting down as a family to watch My Little Pony. Not that Dad looked the least bit willing or excited, more like he was determined to hate the show even if football was in it.

I wondered if I should have custom picked two episodes with sports in them, like the Equestria Games storyline. But the first two? All bets were off.

"You're gonna love this, Daddy!" Holly bounced in her seat, far more confident than I was. "It's the best. I bet you'll like Rainbow Dash most."

"Rain. Bow. Dash." He groaned, like saying "rainbow" made him less of a man. "How long is this gonna take?"

Mom rolled her eyes. "The episodes are like twenty-three minutes long—you'll survive."

"Barely."

I said nothing. I knew I couldn't do anything to convince him. I had to let the show speak for itself. I had to believe in the things that had made me fall in love with it. My Little Pony—it didn't need defending, and I was tired of defending it. Every skeptic in my life who'd watched it—Jake, Emma, Quincy—had seen what I liked about the show. They had accepted me more afterwards.

Either Dad would, or he wouldn't.

The end.

The first episode began with Twilight reading about the return of Nightmare Moon. I glanced at Dad when she was sent to Ponyville to help with the Summer Sun Celebration and ordered to make friends. His face was unmoved, set in an angry glare. I almost waited for him to plug his ears, he looked so annoyed.

As Twilight met her future friends, he didn't betray a single emotion except occasional disgust. I could tell he didn't like Pinkie Pie. Every time she was on-screen his eyes widened, as if the party pony were all his nightmares rolled into one.

I smirked. Now that I thought about it, Pinkie Pie *was* his nightmare.

My dad. Afraid of Pinkie Pie.

It took everything in me not to laugh at the thought, and I couldn't wait to see his face when Pinkie Pie sang the "Laughter Song" at the creepy trees.

"What's so funny?" Holly asked me. Nightmare Moon was about to appear—a completely humorless moment.

"I'll tell you later," I said.

The first episode ended with Princess Celestia disappearing and Nightmare Moon shrouding the world in endless night. We'd made it through half without Dad storming out or complaining too much. Not that this gave me much hope, but I had expected him to mock it a lot more.

Mom stood up. "Oh! The dough! I need to get back to that. Start it without me."

"Okay!" Holly still had the remote clutched to her chest. Maybe she didn't think Dad would make it through two whole episodes before turning on football again. "What do you think, Daddy? It wasn't stupid, was it? It was cool!"

I bit my tongue. If I had asked that, I'm sure Dad would have told me exactly what he thought in the meanest way possible. But with Holly, he forced a smile and said, "Start the next one, baby girl, I don't wanna miss the whole game I was watching."

"Oh, right." Holly pressed PLAY, and we picked up where the first episode ended. Twlight was figuring out what the Elements of Harmony were, and her new friends had come to help her out. Personally, I loved this episode. It was still one of my favorites. Seeing them work together and use their unique talents had always inspired me to be more confident in myself. Maybe I wasn't sporty like Rainbow Dash, but I still had a role to play, a place I belonged.

"You've *got* to be kidding me," Dad grumbled at the dragon and his ruined mustache. I'd forgotten he'd probably hate this even more than Pinkie Pie.

"What?" Holly asked, concerned.

"Nothing," he replied.

Like I expected, the Pinkie Pie song traumatized him, but I noticed that he hadn't hated *all* the parts. He was okay with Applejack saving Twilight, and when Fluttershy tamed the manticore he seemed surprised. Of course, he clearly liked Rainbow Dash and her sportiness and loyalty the most. He almost half-smiled when she turned down a spot with the Shadowbolts.

Mom came back in when they entered the old castle to face Nightmare Moon. "Rolls are rising. Dinner in an hour."

"I really am starving," I said. "I might die by then."

"You'll live." She smiled a little. "If your father can survive this, you can wait an hour for dinner."

Dad didn't reply to the dig. He watched the show, and anger and annoyance turned into something else. Not that it was positive—he just looked plain confused. Twilight gave her speech about discovering the magic of friendship. The Elements of Harmony appeared and defeated Nightmare Moon. Princess Luna appeared in the aftermath and made up with her big sister. Twilight stayed in Ponyville to study friendship, and then it was over.

The credits scrolled by, and we waited for Dad to give his verdict. I tried not to be nervous, but now that his part of the deal had been fulfilled, awaiting the results was excruciating.

"So?" Holly finally said. "Did you like it?"

Dad sighed. He only looked more perplexed as he rubbed the scruff on his chin. I had no idea what he thought, but the lack of an outright declaration of hatred gave me way more hope than it should have. He held out his hand to Holly. "Give me the remote. The game's still going."

Frowning, she did as he said. "But can Drew go to the Brony meet-up or not?"

"Good question," Mom said. "No reason to draw out the suspense."

"I need to think," Dad snapped. "Let me watch the game and get outta my hair."

We scattered out of the living room as quickly as we could. With the future of my social life on the line, I figured for the time being I shouldn't put up a fight. I flopped onto my bed upstairs, exhausted from the arguing and tension that had been building up in our house for a month.

"Can I stay with you?" Holly asked from my doorway.

"Yeah."

She got comfortable next to me, but she wasn't smiling. Holly looked as tired as I felt. She pursed her lips together, and I could tell she wanted to say something but was worried she'd bother me.

"What's up?" I asked.

"It's just . . ." Holly fiddled with her curls, not looking at me. "It really hurt my feelings when Daddy said My Little Pony was stupid."

I sighed. "Me too."

"And then he watched it and didn't even smile once." Her eyes met mine, her face indignant. "How can you not even smile once? He's like Cranky Doodle Donkey, just a big ol' meanie pants."

I laughed. "Oh my gosh, you're so right. He's totally Cranky!"

"We're just trying to be nice to him. Why can't he be nice back?" Holly asked, and I wanted to hug her. For so long I'd seen her as this obnoxious little kid, but she was a lot smarter and more perceptive than we gave her credit for. Much like her beloved My Little Pony.

"Maybe he'll come around eventually," I told her because I couldn't ruin her hopes. Perhaps I wanted to hope a little, too. "Cranky did."

She nodded. "He did, didn't he?"

"Yup." I didn't want to think about this anymore, not when I wanted the answer so badly and couldn't go down there to demand it. So I did the only thing I could to pass the time. "Which pony do you want me to draw?"

Holly perked up. "Do Sunset Shimmer before she got banished! With Princess Celestia!"

"Ooo, good one." I grabbed my sketchpad and got to work. Holly described how she wanted the scene, and I tried to translate that onto the page. I'd gotten a decent pencil outline done when Mom called us down for dinner.

We rushed down, both of us probably eager to find out if Dad had decided yet. And I was so hungry I planned on eating half the food myself. As I took my seat, my mouth watered at the spread—a roast, mashed potatoes, green beans, rolls, and salad. We couldn't say grace fast enough.

". . . Amen," Mom said, and we dug in.

While I shoveled the food into my mouth, I occasionally glanced at Dad. He had gone back to his usual emotionless state and was completely unreadable. I worried he'd never give me an answer just out of spite.

Then Mom cleared her throat. "I think you've had enough time to think, Scott. Time to tell us what you've decided now that you've watched the show."

Dad sighed deeply, and it felt like everything was in slow motion. He wiped his face off with a napkin as slow as a turtle, took a drink from his beer almost as fast as a snail, and when he went for another bite of roast, I lost it.

"Just tell me!" I said. "Can I go or not?"

"No, *you* can't," he said.

I sat back in my chair, reality hitting quickly. Watching My Little Pony . . . it didn't work like I had expected it to. There was the slightest chance it would have, and I'd put more faith in that than I realized. Now it was gone. . . .

"But," he said as he chewed and swallowed. "You *can* take your sister. If she wants to go."

There was a pause, as if none of us quite got what he meant.

"Wait," I said, "so I *can* go?"

"No," he said again, this time more impatiently since I clearly should have understood him. "You can take your sister. She's allowed to go, but she needs a chaperone. You *have to* go—you don't *get to* go. That way me and your mother can go out while you're babysitting her there. That is, if Holly wants to go."

"I wanna go!" She jumped out of her chair. "I really wanna go!"

"There," Dad said, not looking at me or anyone else. "She wants to go, so you have to take her and make sure she's safe. That's what big brothers do."

"Okay . . ." I wasn't entirely sure, but this might have been Dad's way of making things work in his mind. He wouldn't admit outright that he didn't hate My Little Pony or that he approved of me liking it at all. Yet I thought he almost might have, anyway. "So let me get this straight. Holly is allowed to go. I am not, but I have to go with her."

He nodded once. "That's what you say to everyone I know. You only go because you have to take care of your sister. Deal?"

"Deal," I said quickly before he changed his mind.

"Good." He left the table then and went back to his football game. But in his wake he left something new. Not his usual disdain, but a tentative truce. Things might not ever be perfect between me and Dad, but in that moment the winds changed. For the first time in a long while, instead of growing further apart, we'd taken a step towards understanding each other.

I couldn't ask for more than that.

Chapter 38

I STOOD IN front of the school with Skye and Emma waiting for Mrs. Jorgenson to show up with Quincy and Holly. All of us would "chaperone" Holly to the Brony meet-up. I was not allowed to go—I was being forced. My friends thought the whole thing was hilarious, but Skye was happy regardless of my father's stubborn ways.

But first we had a cake to make.

"There they are." I pointed to Mrs. Jorgenson's white van. Most of her kids had left the nest, but she still drove it anyway. Good thing, because we'd fit easily.

"Sweet," Skye said. "No walking at least once a month."

Emma snorted. "We are so spoiled."

"Just wait until we can drive," I said as Mrs. Jorgenson pulled up to the curb. Quincy smiled like a fool, and then he winced and turned around, probably embarrassed. Holly waved frantically from the back seat. She had totally hit the jackpot with this, being at the center of the pony fun now.

I slid the van door open, motioning for the girls to get in first. They went in back and I took the seat by Holly.

"Oh my gosh I *love* your ears!" Holly started right in. "Drew said you make them yourself. Is that true? Can I wear one? Pinkie Pie ones?"

Skye beamed. "Sure. You must be Holly."

"Oh, yeah. Hi." She blushed, a bit starstruck by my friends. She looked at Emma, who clutched her newest book to her chest. "And you're Emma, huh."

Emma nodded. "Nice to meet you, Holly."

"Hey, hey!" Quincy called from the front. "What about me?"

Skye leaned forward, and I could have sworn she was checking him out. "So you really *do* have a friend named Quincy. I was starting to wonder if you were making him up."

"Like an imaginary friend?" Emma laughed.

I glared at them. "You guys think I'm that pathetic?"

"I'm definitely real," Quincy said. "I might even be coming to school here next semester, so you may want to get used to me."

"Okay, okay, everyone," Mrs. Jorgenson said. "You'll have plenty of time to talk once I get to Skye's place, but I need her to tell me where to go first."

"Right!" Skye pointed out the correct streets, and we were at her house in under five minutes.

Mrs. Jorgenson was nice enough to chauffeur us even when she knew she would spend most of the day at a stranger's house and a Brony party. Hopefully, she'd get along with Ms. Zook and it'd be perfect.

We got out of the car, and Emma immediately pulled away to walk the rest of the way home. I hated seeing her go, so I followed her. "Hey."

She jumped, twirling around. "Oh, hey!"

"Your mom doesn't get home for a couple hours, right?" I gulped, suddenly feeling like everyone was looking at us like a couple or something. "Why don't you just come with us? It won't be as fun without you."

"Drew . . ." She looked over my shoulder at everyone, and I swore longing was in her eyes. "You can't help but push me, can you?"

I shrugged. "Sorry."

She sighed and a smile crept onto her lips. "Don't be. Let's go make a cake."

"Yay!" Skye skipped over and hugged her. "Stay with us *forever*."

"Not forever. Though, can you at least save me a piece?"

"Of course!"

Emma came with us to Skye's house, and we got to work on the rainbow cake. Maybe my father would have cringed at the sight of us talking about ponies and baking, but my friends smiled and laughed and had fun. I didn't have just one friend; I had a whole bunch, which was precisely what my parents had hoped for. Precisely what I hadn't dared believe possible.

And all because of a show about ponies and friendship.